THE WAY TO NOD :
Short stories and novelettes by Edan Benn Epstein

Copyright 1993, 2005, 2015

1

THE WAY TO NOD : Short stories and novelettes by Edan Benn Epstein

CHAD

  Calvin was thirty-nine when he decided to leave for an indefinite time. One day he was merely sitting in his comfortable chair when it suddenly occurred to him that a decision had already been made. He would go. Far away. He would begin preparing at once, just as soon as he rose from his chair.

  Up until that moment, Calvin had made a steady if unglamorous living as a technical writer of sorts. Prior to that, he had been a stock clerk in a convenience store, a night manager in an insignificant sandwich shop, and finally an assistant manager in an unvisited bookstore. There was no reason for leaving any job just as there was no reason to stay. Each job paid a little bit more and required just a little bit less. Each job was a little quieter.

  One night, out of pure idleness, he called the toll-free number of a government jobs line. He had found the number on the back page of a newspaper lying on the sidewalk. After several minutes of playing with the automated attendant he listened to a litany of job titles, most of them clerical or administrative. Tiring of this and about to hang up, he was suddenly struck by the mention of an opening for a "Fruit and Vegetable reporter". How sweet, he thinks, amused. So he leaves his name and address asking for an application for the position of Fruit and Vegetable reporter.

  Three days later he receives a large manila envelope. The job requires a college degree and a writing sample, but "prior experience in fruit and vegetable reporting is optional." To his great surprise, he is contacted for an interview and after various bureaucratic rituals with grayish recruiters he is offered the job. His duties include interviewing growers and writing reports on price trends, yields, acreage, pests, distribution, and the like. It occurs to him that had the job been entitled Produce Reporter, he might never have applied. Indeed, he is proud to call himself the Fruit and Vegetable reporter.

  The job rarely requires him to step outside the piss yellow walls of the government building where he writes his reports five days a week. After work, Calvin often strolls through the produce aisles of the

3

supermarket. He enjoys the piped instrumental music and the mist dispensers that keep the produce moist and shiny. Fruits and vegetables are not really food to him. Not really. They are lovely and colorful objects and sometimes he fondles and stares at them, pretending that tonight he will buy them, but he never does. Instead he eats cheese burgers, cokes, and chili fries.

Time passes and the job seems as if it were the only one he had ever had. Yet through some obscure turns of events, Calvin changes assignments. Deep down though, he continues to think of himself as a Fruit and Vegetable reporter. His new position requires him to compile and edit bits and pieces of government almanacs and safety procedure manuals. Tiring of this, he later joins a public utility company to write and edit their glossy leaflets that accompany all their residential invoices. The job is considered very prestigious since his writing is briefly seen and tossed by hundreds of thousands of residents throughout the county. Though Calvin would never be rich, the work pays the bills.

He had always gotten along with everyone at work, which means that he never quarrels with anyone, nor troubles anyone at all by speaking or approaching other people for any reason at all. Once, however, he became friendly with an owl-eyed computer technician named Joel, a man who had once fixed Calvin's computer. One day in the cafeteria, while Calvin stares at an orange, he hears his name. He looks over to see that Joel is waving him over to his table. They begin to eat lunch together every day. Though they rarely actually speak, Joel regards the two of them as friends and one day he invites Calvin to play chess with him in the employee lounge. They are evenly matched and they begin to play several days a week together.

One day, Calvin declines an invitation to play chess and the next day he decides to eat lunch early by himself. The following day, Calvin eats lunch at the diner across the street. After that, Calvin continues to nod and smile at Joel as he passes him in the hallway until one day he realizes that Joel is no longer nodding or smiling back, thus relieving him from the obligation to smile himself any longer.

As the years pass, and as he puts more and more words on paper, he feels less and less the need to ever speak. Few people even know he is still there and are often surprised when they discover that he is.

Calvin takes the bus to work one day while his car is being repaired. He begins to study a woman sitting across from him when he is

4

suddenly convinced that he recognizes her from grade school. The years had not been kind to her nor had she been beautiful to begin with. He remembers her name as Cathy and that she had smiled shyly at him once and that he thought that she must have been of lower social status in school than even he was. And so it seems natural enough for him to reintroduce himself to her. The woman on the bus scowls at first yet he boldly persists in asking for her phone number so that they might get together to discuss "old times." Still scowling, she tears off a tiny scrap of paper from an envelope in her purse and scribbles her name and number.

Her name in fact is Barbara, not Cathy. Calvin and Barbara, indeed, had never gone to school together and had been perfect strangers to each other on the day that they met on the bus. Though she shows little enthusiasm at receiving his call and little more during their first date at a coffee shop, she nevertheless agrees to come back to his apartment where they immediately become lovers. Though she shows little sign of enjoying him, the experience of having sex with someone else is on the whole much better than having it alone.

The next day is dreamlike and the day after that, Calvin feels sad without knowing why. Two weeks later he calls her. She comes and she sits across from him on the couch and she lights a cigarette and they stare at each other. After a mirthless chuckle she puts out the cigarette, yawns and rises. Calvin assumes she is leaving but instead she walks into his bedroom. Every week on Tuesday nights they meet like this for several months. One day, however, she arrives wearing a brand new blouse and make up. She smiles more and she tries to laughs with him and they kiss more than usual and snuggle afterwards. The next day, Calvin resolves to break it off with her, seeing that the relationship has run its course.

Over the next few years he meets several other women while riding the bus which he sometimes chooses to ride even when his car is in good working order. One day, while walking through a junkyard, he meets Jackie, the junkyard owner, an older, creased and wizened chain smoking alcoholic. Having descended the bus at a random stop, Calvin found himself walking amongst her ruins during a rare pique of conscious melancholy. When Jackie asks him to state his business, he confesses he has no business. She laughs and tells him that if reason is all he lacks that she can give him plenty. They make love on a creaky cot in the back of her office, surrounded by empty beer cans, the glare of floodlights and the vision of heaping, crusty stacks of rusted metal set against the pistol black sky.

While still seeing Jackie, Calvin meets Ernestia, who turns out to be the "love of his life" of sorts. Ernestia works as a housekeeper for the gas company. She is a plump, sweet Filipina woman whose husband suddenly leaves her and their six year old daughter to return to the Philippines where he already has another wife and children. Chastely, Calvin and Ernestia date for over a month before they became intimate; the moment they do, she begins to speak immediately of marriage.

Calvin does not wish to marry her, but he likes her very much because she is sweet and wants to take care of him and because her little girl is very well behaved. He does not know what to do. At this same time, Calvin buys a computer with plans to begin working exclusively from home. Ernestia is delighted for it means that Calvin can pick up his little girl from school and give her a glass of milk and see that she stays out of trouble. A man around the house. Calvin lets Ernestia into his life a little bit more each day. It is easy to be with her. She smiles and strokes his thinning hair. She pokes his belly playfully to tease him because he is gaining weight, but then she rubs it gently and kisses it to show him that she really likes it. He likes to feel her hot breath whispering in his ear in her native Tagalog, especially when they are naked together in the dark. Calvin isn't sure what Ernestia sees in him.

The day he starts working from home is the day he begins forgetting to return her phone-calls. Calvin's reputation at the utility affords him many referrals and he has plenty of work every day and evening. When he is not working he plays with the internet and he soon discovers how to begin to "chatting" with women on-line. He assumes that no one is using their real names and he so he never gives away his own. Instead he shares many stories about himself that he makes up as he goes along. Calvin is free to be who he wants to be or needs to be for that moment. He has cyber relationships with different women and he even has occasion to act as multiple personas to the same woman, all from the comfort of his chair. He counsels a married woman in Pennsylvania to leave her husband and to come and stay with him while she sorts out her new life, for it is clear to him that she no longer loves him. One day, the woman announces to him that indeed she has left her husband and is ready to come to him. Calvin immediately ceases his correspondence with her. He sleeps a great deal over the next few days,

6

vowing to avoid his computer, but using it nonetheless with a queasy kind of comfort.

The day will soon approach for him to decide to go far away.

The world inside his living room, with his computer, he knows it is not real. Now suddenly it is no longer enough. Calvin wants to live and it irritates him, this inconvenient realization.

If nothing else Calvin has shaped his life to be convenient. He is able to live well within his means, rarely having to leave his apartment. His food and other necessities are delivered to him, and he requires little. He speaks with clients by phone when necessary, but conducts most of his business on-line.

His greatest crisis is when his computer needs repair. One day, he must let a technician into his apartment to work on his phone line. To prepare, Calvin thrusts all his detritus into the bedroom and is suddenly appalled by the quantity of papers, clothing, and unaccounted for items that suddenly litter his every step, appalled as if he were seeing it all for the first time. When he throws open the windows to let in the outside air, he is dismayed at the sight of a thin, cloying layer of dust that seems to brood upon and corrupt all things. When the technician arrives he resentfully avoids all eye contact, as if the man were not in fact really there at all.

One day the phone rings and it is Calvin's mother. He finds it difficult to say anything. He speaks to her in a dead-flat voice and he all but hangs up on her. This brief conversation, especially with his own mother, disconcerts him considerably. He cannot recall the previous time they had spoken and though they had never really been close, the notion that she was his own "mother" had seemed vaguely important. It occurs to him that it may have been days or even weeks since he has spoken to another human being. The phone rings yet again and he lets it ring and ring. It stops. Then it starts again and he grabs it, refusing to say Hello. A woman sobs quietly on the other end. He feels cold. "Mother?" But it is Ernestia. He listens to her cry for several minutes.

"Why? Why do you not call me anymore? Why do you not care for me anymore?"

He says nothing but he owes it to her to listen. He listens to her and to his own breathing and soon he is listening to random thoughts in his head, including the unwashed dishes in his sink. At last he tells her, "I don't know." Then finally he gently, ever so gently hangs up the

7

phone, as if she had never called at all. Then he unplugs it.

He turns off his computer. He even turns off the fan at his desk and he simply sits for uncounted minutes in his armchair in the darkness of the unlit late afternoon silence. At first there is only hardness and a chilly wind inside of him. He had only intended to sit long enough to get his bearings. His mind is very loud but it says nothing to him. He feels fidgety and uncomfortable, but he stubbornly remains seated in the discipline of nothing. After a long time he begins to listen for the smallest things. He becomes aware of cars passing every few seconds down his street. The tiny sound of a neighbor's television slips discreetly inside his room. Outside, the lonesome song of the ice cream truck mildly chimes outside. Calvin begins to sob. It is as if he is watching a stranger cry and it is both odd and revolting to him.

This too passes. And still he sits.

Then he hears it. Instantly he recognizes the sound of a fork settling closer to the bottom of a pot he had used to boil some rice for lunch yesterday. This little noise cheers him at first, but then saddens him in the most impersonal way. He thinks about it, remembering it, precisely because it was the sort of thing that was meant to go unnoticed or at least once noticed quickly become entirely forgotten. He looks around the room as if he were looking to see what was going on, as if anything was going on. He has a profound awareness that he is just sitting there, sitting around, doing nothing whatsoever, not even daydreaming, not even sleeping, nor meditating, but simply doing nothing whatsoever. He now senses correctly that he is only moments away from making his decision. It will not be long before he forgets the phone calls from his mother and from Ernestia; years later, however, he will still remember the fork. Only the fork. Everything that shall come to pass will do so only because an ordinary random fork in his sink has settled a few inches deeper inside a pot full of dirty water and because Calvin had been silent enough to hear it as it happened.

He rises at last from his chair, feeling as though he is watching someone else. Outside it is nearly dark. He had been sitting in his chair for several hours but now at last he stands on his feet. He stands wondering what to do. Finally he ventures shyly outside. He walks around the block in the cool early evening haze and then he walks around the block again.

A decision has been made. He is about to change everything, if

8

only because he could and perhaps because he can no longer possibly do otherwise. It occurs to Calvin that his decision had already been made from the moment he heard the fork settle in his sink.

He begins his planning that very night. Because he takes pride in his work, he decides he will complete assignments for which he had already accepted money. Calvin refuses additional assignment requests that come through his email. He informs all of his clients through email that there has been a sudden death in the family and he gives no further explanation. In retrospect, he considers that even this terse fabrication is more than he needed to say.

There is only the manner of arranging access to all his bank accounts from wherever he is. He cancels his accounts, then he sells the computer itself, most of his furniture (for very little money, and what he couldn't sell, he simply abandons). All this he achieves in merely three days. Only the money remains.

And his car. He keeps his car, of course, his nine year old Camry, reliable, durable, dull. He changes the oil and checks the tires and brakes. On the morning of the fourth day following the incident with the fork in the sink, he sits drinking tea at his kitchen table enjoying the wooly, quiet morning. The couch is gone, but a single soft chair remains. The computer is gone. That was the biggest change and Calvin feels its goneness. Now there is nothing else to focus on, nothing else to demand or absorb attention. Nothing exists but the aloneness of a few scattered and inconsequential things. Calvin checks his watch and before he even realizes it, he takes his apartment key off of his key chain and he puts it on the table. He takes a last look through his closet and drawer, and he fills his duffle bag with comfortable clothes.

He slings the bag over his shoulders and dumps it in the trunk of his car, slamming it shut. It's an unusually wintry gray day in early June in Los Angeles. Calvin sighs and gets in the car, turns the key and listens to the engine idle for a minute. For a moment he thinks about getting out to take one last look at his apartment, but the key is already locked inside, and it is truly only an empty shell. It is no longer his home.

Ω

It is just past ten in the morning when he enters the 10 freeway heading east and this direction surprises him for he had thought of heading north but the car decides to head east instead. So Calvin decides he will follow his car. He meets little resistance as he heads through downtown, past the choked and sooted warehouse district and on past the velveteen hillsides festooned with little pink and yellow drabble houses. Calvin continue past the isolated ghetto republics of the east side though a vast increasingly flat and attenuated plain of corporate parks, mega malls, and franchised yuppie eateries. All these he leaves behind before the noon hour. On he drives past the thin, down, smoky ribbons of San Bernardino, finally entering a region of rolling, golden knolls and brush, the freeway leavening out, lanes falling away, radio stations coughing and winking. Shortly after passing a sign for Moreno Valley, Calvin pulls over at a roadside eating spot. The dust kicks up as Calvin pulls into the dirt, rutted lot. Calvin has the generic patty melt with oily coffee.

He looks out toward the highway and listens to the rumbling eighteen wheelers, bulky mastodons shaking through the day. By nightfall he has already traversed the sage filled California desert, distant low-lying shelves of rock peaking near the horizon. He crosses the border unceremoniously into Arizona and passes one small, often destitute hamlet and truck-stop after another. He keeps driving, stopping only for gas, stretching out his doughy legs and sweaty bottom, remembering what it's like to walk upright. For dinner he slows down to pass through a fried chicken take-out then continues past a succession of decrepit motels. Finally he pulls over in the middle of the night and he gratefully finds his room amongst a squat collection of bungalows close to the highway.

The bed is stiff, almost lumpy and it creaks with every frequent roll of his restless body. Everything is decorated in the most perfunctory way. There is a television without a remote and no telephone at all. The act of turning a heavy clicking knob on a television seems almost rococo, antiquated, as if he were visiting some Soviet style industrial sticking-set east of the Urals. He turns the channel dial, thinking one way then another, turning the dial. But the television is off.

10

In the morning, Calvin is awakened by thunking car doors and by feet scraping across the gravel lot, a man's phlegm ridden cough scanning past his door. Life from the highway has picked up again. Nasal voices chatter and whine outside in desultory fashion, punctuated by the ever louder hawking of a spooning gob of nicotine mucous, quivering upon the pavement. Calvin opens an eye resentfully, disgusted at this image, wondering if he can avoid spying or stepping upon such a graceless calling card, or indeed, any trace of this loathsome family. For an interminable period it seems, Calvin feels subjected to their idle chatter, coughing and spitting, and other evidence of their bodily orifices. And suddenly, Calvin feels his gut tighten and burn in an unfamiliar way. He curses them in his mind. They should all be stricken in mid reflection of breakfast and their lifeless corpses ground into fertilizer! How many fucking car doors have to slam? Don't they know to open a door and leave it open until they have finished loading? Shut up you worthless brats! Calvin surrenders himself utterly to his mental tantrum. He envisions himself strangling the unseen children.

Mercifully, the car, which is right outside his door, finally whirs into life. Yet Calvin's exquisite torture is still not an end. For the engine proceeds to idle endlessly, panting its exhaust. How long will he have to endure this pointless drone before these worthless beings put the damn thing into gear and drive away? He imagines the idle dropping, tires crunching over gravel, wistfully fading into the welcoming distance, his curses following them all the way out.

And at last his wish comes true and the car begins to leave, and just as Calvin invects his malediction upon them a final time, just at that precise moment, indeed he starts at the muscular blast of a mammoth freight truck just before detonating into a mangled crash across his ears, strafing the road, groaning and thundering down the highway.

Calvin leaps out of bed, stumbles to the window and pulls back the curtain, but he can see nothing, only the scrambling of the office manager and numbers of guests running toward the disaster. Calvin too, throws a shirt on and some pants and struggles to put his shoes on. He puts a hand on the door knob but freezes, unable or unwilling to turn it. He strains to hear the gasps of the on-lookers, a voice or two rising above the others, loudly lamenting "Call an ambulance!" or simply, "Sweet Jesus!". Heavy feet and jangling keys rush past his door again. Calvin flattens his ear against the paint splintered door and slowly his knees begin to sink until he is all but lying against it, arms held tight around his chest, breathing heavily. Above his head, the door explodes in furious knocking, pushing his heart and breath away from him. He is being called out. Found out. Any moment a key will be inserted in the door and he'll be dragged out across the pavement. A voice high above him, tinny compared to the heavy hand on his door shouts out, "Is there a doctor, a medic?" Next door the knocking resumes. Calvin remains fixed in his slump, ear to his own door. "Anybody a doctor or a medic!" the voice shouts more shrilly.

Another voice replies, "Don't bother. Don't bother."

"Fucking Christ!" the first one says, voice breaking.

"Don't bother. Don't bother" the other one repeats, stupidly, his voice broken. Finally, the ambulance announces its arrival. Calvin discovers he is still hunched on the floor, his ear against the door. Stiffly he rises and checks the clock. To his surprise it is only ten minutes past eight. He calculates he has nearly three hours before he has to vacate the room. He turns the air-conditioning on high and attempts a fitful sleep. Somehow he reasons he cannot leave until they clean that mess outside.

At half past ten, Calvin takes his shower. The soap, he notices for some reason, appears unused but is also unwrapped and sits and waits for him lonely inside the shower stall. The hissing water is surprisingly strong and plenty hot.

Outside it is quiet. He peeks out from behind his curtain and he sees the manager sweeping out the front step. At all costs he wishes to avoid encountering anyone seeing him leave the room. He opens the door, pokes his head through and hauling his duffle bag, he takes three or four quick steps. Then turns around once then twice as if to lose the bearings of anyone who might happen to see him and think, 'Oh look, there's someone we thought just left his room, but I guess we were mistaken because he just turned around so he must be just going about his business and happens to find himself here, with no knowledge whatsoever of this recent carnage.'

Twenty feet or less to reach his Camry.

He scrambles in and turns the engine over. Through his rear view mirror he can see the manager, a big gawk of a man, look up and frown in his direction. Calvin quickly puts the car in gear and it

hiccoughs and then dies. Through the mirror, Calvin sees the man lean
on his broom, still looking at him. He turns the key and it whinnies and
whinnies but the engine won't start. Through the mirror, the manager
puts his broom down and slowly starts to walk toward the car. Damn it,
damn it, Calvin insists through his teeth, and the curse actually seems to
bring the car back to life. What is all of this to me? I am not even here.
I am always just passing through. The car lurches into gear in reverse,
yelping like a wounded puppy, and the manager stops in his tracks.
Calvin backs out and takes a glancing shot at the front bumper of a Ford
pick-up parked to his left. As he turns the wheel now to face the street,
the manager is still walking toward him on his left, now glancing at the
pick-up truck and just as the man sharply hails him, Calvin puts the car
in drive and forwards across the gravel to the road.

The road is blissfully empty and he takes his foot off the brake
preparing to turn right and towards the future. Blue crystal shards of
broken glass shimmer on the cusp of the road facing the driveway. The
manager still stands in his rearview mirror, still frowning, stopped still.
Suddenly the man starts running towards him. Calvin hits the accelerator
and the tires squeal and he jolts out onto the road and all at once he is
free and at peace and the motel driveway disappears forever.

There is nothing ahead of him but limitless miles, freedom,
though the thought of it elicits a nauseous shudder. He settles in for the
straight shot across New Mexico. Along the way appear dozens of
peculiar points upon the desert where he might stop and wander off to
disappear. On and on he drives. Before sundown he enters the broad
cactus dotted plain of west Texas. As night falls, his stomach growls and
knots for he hasn't eaten all day, so he pulls over at a dilapidated
roadside eaterie.

He looks inside, askance at the busy plates full of dire looking
steak remnants, mashed potatoes, and obscene globbings of brinish
gravy. Rolled up flannel sleeves reveal hirsute, meaty arms, synthetic
caps bearing the name of their auto shop, trucker's union, John Deere, or
the NRA. He fixates on the caps rather than on the faces wearing them,
as if the caps were wearing the faces. For an odd moment his eyes lock
with those of a wide bodied hatless hulk whose furry flat top carpets his
belvedere head. Calvin blinks and turns away. He thinks again of the
accident.

That night he finds a suitable yet remote and homely looking inn. Simple, clean, efficient. Before going to bed he circumambulates the little motel twice, looking up often at the whirlwind glaze of stars pressing down upon him through the black depth sky. He lays down, exhausted. Over and over he sees the accident in a series of dreams, which he had never seen with his eyes. The last of these dreams is the most disturbing, for there is nothing but darkness and he simply hears it again, every subtle scratch and groan of metal and shatter of glass, almost as in slow motion. As he strains to compulsively listen each time, he wonders if this or that metallic scream might not instead be human, doomed to relive its own death inside of Calvin's lest it perish forever unheard. Calvin awakens at dawn, his heart racing, angry and determined to leave this matter behind him.

During the next night he passes relentlessly through San Antonio and Houston. He glances at glass giant spires, glinting in the moonlight. He sleeps in his car. Somewhere near Mobile, Alabama, his car overheats on a back road. Calvin walks the nearly five difficult miles to the nearest town to find a mechanic to come out and tow his car. Everything about this land exudes heat and moisture. Everything, including himself seems to move more slowly as though through plasma. The mechanic has asquare bedrock of a face, solid in this liquid feel of a land, his red hands and fingers tuberous, clean of fresh grease but etched with minor cuts and oil creased callouses. He wears baggy grime streaked jeans and a workman's shirt the color of dried blood, the name Jarvis stitched on the front. He tells Calvin to return by a certain hour when he will have fixed what turns out to be a busted water hose. Jarvis asks him, "Do you know where you are now?"

"No," says Calvin, with no indication that he is interested. The man wipes his hands on a filthy rag and says nothing more. So Calvin wanders languorous slow through the little town, swampy green, dust flaked; wanders in and out of tobacco fumed convenience stores, past churches and little shaded houses with meticulous tiny lawns, facing streets without side-walks. He passes the time at a tiny park, hot and sweaty, numbed, yet suddenly anxious, as though there were something that needed to be done, something important that he was forever putting off. He looks at the slender trees and a breeze breaks the monotony and raises the brushing of branches and leaves all around him. Though he is eager to be rid of this place, he nevertheless imagines what it would be

14

like to stay here forever, with nothing to do and nowhere to go and nothing ever expected of him.

After paying the mechanic, Calvin revs the engine and continues on, fretting whether the mechanic truly fixed his car, or whether the gaskets would blast or the radiator would suddenly geyser, his car bleeding angry black smoke. Finally he loses himself for silent hours on subtle interchange turn-outs. He winds south toward Miami. There, between the beach front and the port, Calvin turns onto an obscure used car dealer lot. There, underneath the heavy Florida butter sun and the colorful day, Calvin sells his Camry to a slender Jamaican dealer in a cheap Seersucker suit for $400 cash, barely more than it cost to fix it. But he feels as light as a feather.

He hires a cab to the port and knocks around the docks and the shipping office, shyly managing to inquire about destinations and whether he could pay for a no frills passage to some place far, far away. They stare at him for a bit and shake their heads, saying that all the ships they handle are freighters, not cruise ships, but then they shrug and tell him that if he can talk to the captain of any ship, he may have a chance. But they say nothing more. Calvin walks out and wanders, thinking of Jamaica or even South America since it is relatively easy to find ships that will go there. But in the end it is not far enough. He wants a long journey drifting across the glassy water between the edges of the world.

At last he manages to introduce himself to a roving steward who shrugs his shoulders and introduces Calvin to a fire-plug of a Greek captain who looks at him cock-eyed, stroking his bristling beard with a curious thumb and forefinger, and finally, chuckling mirthlessly to himself, he tells Calvin that he will take him on, that they have a light crew to manage a precious undisclosed cargo. They leave early the next morning for the port of Dakar in Senegal. Africa. "Don't bother offering me cash. Your fare will be to accompany the purchasing agent into town tonight to assist him in buying our food-stuffs," he winks "You of course will eat what we eat at meal times, but of course you may bring anything you want for yourself. This is a ten day voyage. Make sure you have a warm jacket, just in case, and bring lots of Dramamine and sunblock. Bring your own bedding as well. We're not a hosteller you know, nor a nursing facility. You've never been to sea before? Of course not. Why are you doing this? No, don't tell me. You just want to be far away. Is that it? Hmm. Far away. Yes. Well, you will certainly be that. You will

15

certainly be plenty of that," he repeats, his voice trailing off. "Bring your passport, of course."

And Calvin joins the Filipino ensign, a soft spoken ageless and slender man. They make their purchases, using Calvin's money. Cigarettes. Coffee. Vodka. Potatoes, powdered milk, and lots and lots of canned foods. The ensign smiles shyly at this purpose, explaining needlessly that the captain and his crew need their vodka. Calvin purchases cheap comfortable clothing, paperbacks, snack-foods, cheap bedding, sunblock and Dramamine. They eat silently together at a small, Chinese restaurant with a large aquarium, Calvin surprisingly at ease with the pleasant silence between them. Briefly, he imagines a modern world of convenience, sparsely populated with politely silent, gentle individuals like this nameless ensign across from him. Then he remembers Ernestia and feels a vague longing, though not necessarily to be with her again.

They arrive back at the ship at after dark, Calvin hauling his overstuffed duffle-bag, the ensign genially and comfortably laden with far more than looked possible for him to carry. The ship is a mammoth metal husk, its deck the length of a football field, illuminated by industrial lights cast from towering stacks. A great crane wheezes and hums like some great extinct creature, lowering one of dozens of trailer sized plastic drums of unnamed substances into the black depths of the cargo holds. The port is ablaze with nocturnal activity aboard dozens of ships. The ensign escorts Calvin, climbing down narrow flights of stairs to find his room, a narrow but passable living space. No desk or chair. Just a bunk with a metal bar to prevent the sleeping soul from being ejected to the floor during the heaving sighs upon choppy waters. Calvin settles in, somnolent and pleasantly numb.

The ship leaves at four in the morning. Calvin misses both breakfast and lunch that first day, sleeping fitfully in his little bunk. No one attempts to rouse him. He asks the ensign when he should arrive for dinner, then sheepishly makes his appearance. There he is given a terse exclamatory greeting from the crew before sitting down. Eight men are seated, including himself, a skeleton crew for such a large ship. They sit around a long mess table, the meal a bowl of bland tomato soup with a spongy chunk of grayish bread.

Calvin meets the crew twice a day for meals but he mostly eats what he had wisely brought for himself; tins of spam and sardines and

16

crackers, generously estimating his needs for ten days with nothing to distract himself but his books and his snacks. He likes the sound that the metal top makes when the ring peels foaming back to reveal the viscera of steaming spam beneath, resembling nothing so much as cat food mixed with disgorged blood from a slashed finger.

He finds the ship superbly supportive of his splendid isolation. He stretches his legs and walks the deck, sniffing about. Surrounding him on every side is the limitless lonely blue ocean. The further the ship moves upon the featureless waters, the more carefully etched the heavens above become, and he wanders on deck at night, despite warnings of falling overboard, even in still weather. He contemplates the boiling ocean and the waxing and waning of the brilliant moon.

When the ensign is on duty in the engine room, Calvin visits him and asks him questions about the dimly lit maps and charts upon the walls and tables. Tiny green lights splay on the control panel. Lighted sky above and sky like pitch below. Although the crew stays in the upper decks, Calvin's quarters are below where he also spends much of his time. Often he wanders slowly past the steamy gray engine room, just to listen to the huge heaving of the giant furnaces. Having brought an ample supply of paperbacks, he reads for hours on end, punctuated by narcoleptic naps. He eats in his room and is as content as he can ever remember. This ship demands nothing from him and the crew leaves him alone, though the captain smirks and grumbles in his presence. The remaining humans are perfect in number to provide the decorative reassurance of safety, while at no time imposing upon his person. It is as if they functioned solely for his benefit and modest comfort, yet without doing a thing directly for him other than discharging their normal duties at a comfortable distance.

It isn't until the fifth night that they run into choppy waters and the ship begins to heave at unlikely lengths and angles. Calvin regrets not taking his precautionary dose of Dramamine, straining to even retch properly inside his tiny toilet, though there was no longer much to retch. Much later, the ensign finds him crouched in the fetal position posed in a corner of the swaying room. Calvin remembers a fizzing glass presented to him, a warm sinewy brown hand steadying his shoulder, even a good humored, gentle chuckling from the direction of where his friend must be. I must have dreamed you up, Calvin thinks. Again he remembers Ernestia, for she too is Filipina. Let's go to the Philippines, Calvin says

17

to himself, only he must have said it out loud, for now his friend is beaming at him and saying, No No, You go to the Philippines another day my friend. But now you're going to a place much more far, far away. Calvin closes his eyes and sees the stars in the sky, moving faster than they ought. His lower organs twist to the motion of the creaky cabin. Though he fights to stay motionless, the world is unhinged and there are no fixed points. So how does his friend stand it, pill or no pill? Friend? Calvin hears himself refer to the ensign as his friend, the word exotic in his head. Then he is led to his bunk and he can hear the metal barrier sliding into place, rattling his brain. He feels the blanket placed squarely upon him, tucked in snug at the corners, and he feels himself relax. Did the man carry him or did he somehow walk on his own? He makes a mental note that he must thank his friend when he feels better. But the man, invisible now save for his tawny brown hands, is already saying, No problem, No problem, you welcome, you welcome. You rest now, you rest. Sleep now. You sleep. And his words sound both ridiculous and convincing.

The next two days are a timeless blur, fathomed only in retrospect. He forces down a little iced tea, a few dry crackers. His stomach feels as miserably small and dry as the crunched out corner of a discarded card-board box. When finally he recovers and staggers out on deck upon rickety legs, squinting into the glare, he feels like a guest upon the planet. Gradually all normal feeling returns.

The ship docks at the port of Dakar just after sunrise. The musky African coast is lit coral and cream when the city comes into view. "OK, then. You are here now. Are you ready?" his only friend says smiling at him. But looking into his eyes, he saw sadness in them, and it annoyed him, judging that the ensign knew in his heart that Calvin wasn't at all ready for what was to come. Or that it was all a horrible mistake.

"As ready as I am ever going to be," he boasts, truthfully, a little louder than necessary. "Are you coming also? Just to get off the ship for the day?"

"No, no. I don't bother leaving the ship anymore. There is nothing any longer for me to see," he says with perfect contentment. Calvin wonders whether his friend simply meant he no longer went ashore at foreign ports, or if in principle he had chosen never to leave the

18

ship ever again for any reason. For there was nothing to see anywhere, anymore. Only later did Calvin remember that he and the ensign had both gone shopping together for foodstuffs back in the states. Calvin wonders how much else he'd soon have difficulty remembering and if he'd even mind.

He takes a moment to remember to take everything he needs, double checking his papers, his passport, his credit cards as well as his few possessions. After wandering a long time through the port, secretly terrified, trying to ignore a surprising number of eager stares and nods, he finds a taxi, a man driving an old Thunderbird convertible who takes him straight to the heart of the ramshackle busy city. No one asked for his passport. Here he was a complete stranger.

The hotel he chooses wedges narrowly in the gutter like street, an obscure alley in the main of town. He is given a church key and he wanders up the creaky steps to the fourth floor where he finds a sink and rusty faucet, lacy curtains, and French windows. He keeps the windows open, and at all hours he hears people talking and laughing and distant music and the smell of fried food wafts inside. He lies there not knowing what to do with himself and more restless than he can remember. Irritated with himself, he misses the ship and its simple, undemanding routines, its dull days and quiet nights. He misses his friend, the ensign, whose name it astonishes him he cannot recall and perhaps never knew.

After an initial depression, he finds to his surprise and delight, however, that the strangeness of his earthly surroundings quickly become familiar and appropriate, and the days began to quickly roll past as he becomes accustom to the minor inconveniences of the life of a man of moderate means with no particular business in an African city. Since he has nowhere to be and no obligations to perform, he gives himself to the restless heat and to wandering, lost amongst narrow, filthy alleys, and suspect market places, past colonial style government offices, or even as far as the port. Always he avoids direct contact with people as though they were merely projections from his subconscious. He moves, endlessly harassed by French speaking natives, yet walking serenely past it all. The cafes are always packed and he remains sitting many an afternoon, content amongst the frenetic but seemingly desultory activity of swarms of people everywhere.

Soon he runs out of books to read and so he reads no more. Instead he walks and he watches. Men with short white sleeves and pitch black skin talk and talk loudly in a cobblestone alley or behind some half abandoned cinder block. Sometimes they gamble with dice shaken from strange cups. There were numerous Europeans and even Americans, women even, and he occasioned their acquaintance, even indulging in major drinking bouts with them. He entered into cordial relations with an Englishman named Lonny, an engineer from Sussex who was on extended holiday. Sometimes they wandered together and Calvin let himself be led toward ill lit hallways where out of the darkness the Englishman procured for them opium and a Vietnamese or Moroccan prostitute. Then they were led to a tiny back room lit by a single lamp and furnished only with cushions whose color was obscured by the thin, oily light. The four of them then lay together and an indefinite period passes. As if articulating a valuable insight, Calvin floats his voice upon the gelatinous silence and speaking presumably to Lonny, he says, "I've been thinking now. Wouldn't it be an advantage somehow if one could live comfortably amidst a world of people who did not speak a single word you understood and who understood nothing of what you said? I mean, might that not be in some ways make one free, presuming you had the money to shake around? I think I should like to live like that," Calvin concludes, forgetting that he already does in fact live exactly like that. The silence greets him, firmly, irrevocably, yet Calvin was sure in the moment that Lonny had heard him.

When the mood strikes him, Calvin visited the lobbies of the finest hotels in search of English speaking tourists with whom he could play the affable role of arm chair tour guide. He even managed to pick up some French and a smattering of German. Of the native people, he knows nothing at all.

One day, he stumbles upon a tiny book store hidden behind an open air market full of strange and misshapen foods. To his surprise, he finds inside a large number of scrolled up maps of Central Africa, places even more remote than where he finds himself now. He pours an outstretched finger over the map of the equatorial continent. Then he spreads his palm across it, admiring its implications of vastness, rubbing the page like the stretched, smooth belly of a gloriously fat woman. Through Senegal, into the increasingly empty region of Mali, then through Niger, until finally piercing into an even larger, more empty country still by the curious name of Chad, as landlocked and alien a region as could be found anywhere on the planet, he suspected. In that

20

very instant he decides he shall travel there directly. Of course. How could I have thought that my movement was finished? Only now can it properly take shape.

Rather than find a series of planes to transport him, Calvin determines to reach Chad by traversing the Sahara, a notion he is fully aware he is as foolishly unprepared for as one could possibly imagine. As if sharing a joke and a wink with an unseen audience, he dismisses any practical concern, declaring to himself instead that it matters not how long it took to get there. Time was of absolutely no consequence. This was why he fit in as well as he had at Dakar, for though surrounded by activity, nothing was done with any sense of urgency or destination. Everything was eternally now all the time. He was merely taking the next logical step in moving towards that eternal now.

Calvin changes money and purchases a bus ticket for Bamako, the capital city of Mali. He boards a dead avocado colored bus, fabric bursting from the upholstery, passengers crowded in the aisles. Calvin had paid first class which simply entitles him to the privilege of boarding first to claim a seat. Since there was is no overhead rack, he carries his duffle bag in his lap, his passport and money shrewdly roped and stowed around his neck, beneath his shirt.

By now, he rarely thinks of his old life, can remember less and less of it anyway. His clearest memory is of being aboard a giant freighter ship. Once upon a time he had lived in a modest yet comfortable apartment and he had communed hour after hour with his computer. He had been a wordsmith, shaping sentences for the sole purpose of documentation. But never for consumption. Whatever he wrote was never to be read. Whereas the weight of all that documentation was formidable, the sense of it was weightless. It was form over substance. So Calvin himself is weightless and this is how he understands his own freedom.

His mind wanders over this grim terrain as the bus jolts its way slowly across the crumbling highway, the shoulders of which are littered with rusted shells of abandoned pick-up trucks. The bus stops frequently, sometimes at the side of the road for no apparent reason. Other times, slender adolescent boys in white short sleeves too big for them board to sell bottles of orange soda and plastic bags of water. The first day out, Calvin remains seated even at village stops, for fear of losing his seat in the tumult. He sleeps in his seat and doesn't eat.

21

Suddenly a shot rings out. No one reacts and it turns out that a tire had blown, stranding the bus on a long particularly desolate stretch of flat road, parched mountains sinister in the distance. Judging from the reactions of the passengers who gathered outside to smoke and socialize, the flat seemed no cause for alarm, and Calvin used the distraction to find cover a few yards away in order to relieve himself. He feels only sad that he had neglected to purchase any toilet paper for the journey. When he returns, several of the passengers have gathered around the driver, laughing and debating on how to repair the flat. Remarkably, the tire is repaired within an hour, and they resume the journey.

Calvin learns to force himself to step down at villages so he can purchase some stew or bread to eat, though not all villages had any food to sell. He takes his duffle bag with him always, but strangely he never bothers to change into his other clothes, indifferent to how soiled his present outfit is already becoming. After the first horrible night, he was able to stretch out in his seat, while some of the other passengers climbed on top of the roof or talked amongst themselves outside long past midnight. When the roads were smooth, life was easier, and he spends much of his days in a pleasant stupor, slumped over his bag, hallucinating as to the meaning of the meaningless words that were spoken around him, even when no one was speaking. Early one morning, the fourth or fifth day, the bus stops at a relatively modern village with shingled roofs, a few cars needlessly honking their horns through the dusty street. Here the driver exchanges buses as if he were changing horses, though the new one hardly looks any better for ware than the previous one.

Calvin sleeps but then awakens to hear his stomach loudly growling. Weary and famished, he descends, experiencing as always that sensation of momentarily feeling only three feet tall when first stepping upon the earth. This time he forgets to take his duffle bag with him, but still, he carries his passport and money, as well as a bag of water in his hand. It was some timeless part of the day beneath the blue pagan sky. He tours the village, feeling depleted yet refreshed to be walking. Young boys, barely six or seven begin running past him and a moment later he realizes they are beginning to run in circles around him. He tries to ignore them.

A man with shiny skin and a mass of jumbled yellow buck teeth, approaches, shooing the boys away. The man then turns to Calvin and begins to speak to him in a language he recognizes as French. Though his first inclination is to ignore the man, Calvin manages to understand that he is being offered a ride anywhere he wishes, in the man's own private car.

As if to underscore his point, the man points towards the bus and shakes his head ruefully. He has one yellowed, bloody eye, the other one clear. Calvin wonders, did someone punch him in the eye, or is he suffering from an infection? Then the intrusively absurd thought seizes him that he should hit this man as hard as he can in the eye that's clear just so he can test the results. For a moment, Calvin wonders if he has said all these thoughts aloud but apparently not so, for the man is still talking, instead of staring at him in alarm. The man proudly takes Calvin to view his vehicle, a rusted military surplus jeep, grinning and preening as though it were a brand new Lexus. Now they are talking money. "Mais ou tu vas? Ou tu vas?" But where are you going? Where are you going? The man's French gets crowded in his teeth. Calvin understands this much all the same.

"Chad!" he declares, sure that the name must be the same in English as in French.

"Quoi? Ou?" What? Where?

"Je vais au Chad. Voila." I'm going to Chad.

The man frowns in comical surprise, his distorted teeth exaggerating his disgust at the incredible pronouncement he has just heard, as if Calvin had just told him he intended to go to Mars. Then he narrows his eyes and nods and finally replies. "Ou tu vas, monsieur?" As if to say, where are you *really* going.

Calvin patiently wipes his brow and repeats, "Je vais au Chad. Chad. OK? Tu connais Chad? C'est la, non?" I'm going to Chad. Do you know Chad? It's over there, no? And he points toward the rising sun.

The man comically squints. Then he grins broadly, nods his head, and winks. "Oui, oui. Chad! C'est la bas, tout loin, tout loin." Yes, Chad, it is over there. It's far, far away. There is a pause and then the man suddenly puffs up and proudly announces, "OK. OK. Pas de probleme. On va au Chad." No problem. We'll go to Chad. Now comes the time to negotiate a price. He advises Calvin to buy as much sorghum, a grain one can cook on the along the way, as well as water, blankets, and more food that will last. Then he gives him directions to a store near

23

the main square. They agree to meet up in two hours at a café next to the store, during which time the man can service his jeep. Then the man insists on payment from Calvin up front for a spare tire and some motor oil. Calvin refuses. I will give you money when we leave and pay you as we go. The man shrugs and seems to agree.

Calvin returns to the bus to retrieve his dufflebag. But the bus has already disappeared. He realizes he is completely indifferent and even a little relieved. Now he has nothing. No change of clothing. But he still has what counts, his passport and his money and he wanders toward the center of the small, yet bustling town. The streets are filled with youths in white cotton shirts, swerving perilously on rusty, ancient looking bicycles, scattering ragged chickens. Out of nowhere, a huge black Mercedes rolls slowly down the boulevard, a man wearing dark sun glasses behind the wheel staring impassively behind his tinted windshield.

He finds the general store, nearly empty of customers, except for a man in a military looking jacket, leaning against an empty shelf, cleaning his teeth with a gold toothpick. He is an especially tall, dark man, powerfully built, clean shaven, eyes glowing from his face. The man looks Calvin up and down as if he wanted to fuck him. And suddenly Calvin feels more vulnerable and shaky than he ever has in his entire life. All at once, this land, this street is not where he wants to be. Where is his long lost room with the computer and where is his cozy job as a fruit and vegetable reporter?

He makes his purchases with a heavy heart, fumbling with the strange currency, looking at the old clerk, who does not return his look, and expecting at any moment to be arrested or shaken down for a bribe. He selects his grimy blankets, bags of rice, water, salt, and several large, unmarked, dusty dark round bottles of what turns out to be off brand rum. The man with the toothpick nods at him and says in a loud, deep, chilling voice, "Est-ce que je peux vous aider, monsieur?" May I help you, sir?

"Non, merci." Calvin replies. What kind of 'help' could he mean?

"You need no help so far from home? Very well. Take care, my friend," the man says in perfect English. He adds, "You know that here you are safe. But you do not want to attract too much attention to yourself in this place."

24

"OK. Thank you. Thank you very much. But I don't need any help with these," Calvin replies unthinking, already sweating with his loads.

"Nor did I offer any. Is this what I offered? Do I look like a porter to you?" the man says indignantly, pulling the toothpick from his mouth.

"God, no sir. I did not think you were a porter." Calvin says.

" 'Sir'. You call me 'sir' now. You are frightened of me?"

"I have to go now, please."

With a flourish, the man gestures towards the half open door. "Then go."

Calvin nods and stumbles past him, somehow managing his purchases. He is half way out when he hears the voice query, "You are American?" But Calvin is going to ignore this question, for there can only be more trouble behind it. Can I make it back to the meeting point without being robbed? he wonders. Suddenly the door slams shut in front of him, and the man in the military jacket is now staring at him, unsmiling. "Answer my question."

"What?"

"You heard me. Are you American?"

Calvin sighs. "Yes..... And?"

"Look at yourself, American." Calvin just looked at the man. "Just you look at yourself. Now you look at me." The man straightens to his full height, over six feet tall He leans forward and says, "Look at you. Now look at me. Now you tell me, American, why is this America of yours so strong, and we are so weak? Do you think that's right? Do you think that makes any sense?"

Calvin opens his mouth. "No," Calvin replies, in all honesty.

The man smiles and continues, "Did you know that you stink? Go take a bath."

"I do stink" Calvin replies, somewhat apologetically.

"All right then my weak, little American friend. You take care, then. And the next time we see each other, you are going to buy me a beer. You understand?"

Calvin walks as quickly as he can down the street toward his meeting point. The man asked Calvin to buy him a beer, but he might as well have said he was going to hunt Calvin down and sodomize him, for all it sounded. He has already walked several blocks when suddenly he

25

realizes that he was supposed to meet the toothy driver at the café right next to the store. What a golden opportunity to buy someone a beer? He drops one of his bags and a man picks it up and hands it back to Calvin and then walks on his way. Where are all the women in this strange town? Calvin thinks. He finds the café and dashes inside, expecting to find his nemesis waiting for him, but the café is nearly empty. Calvin orders a beer for himself and waits.

At last, the toothy man returns, at first insisting that they spend the approaching night in town. But Calvin tells him to drive regardless out of town. The man shrugs, smiles at him, and names a premium price to begin their trek with dusk approaching. Calvin pays, knowing that he'll have to argue with this one about how often and how much. But the important thing, it seems is that they leave, and continue eastward.

It takes forever, it seems, to inch the vehicle through the ever more crowded street. In a flash, then, the town ends and so do nearly all traces of habitation, except for a few mud looking huts and corrugated tin shacks. The road becomes difficult terrain, bumpy and full of rocks and sand. When night finally falls, the road has all but disappeared and the man refuses to drive any further. They sleep that first night on the ground to the side of the road. Calvin does not sleep. He is up casting a suspicious watch over his sleeping driver. He imagines himself stealing and driving off without his guide. Who would miss him? He imagines the man rising up and stealing Calvin's money and passport. Then he imagines the driver creeping towards him with a knife drawn to slit his weak American throat. In fact, here it happens now, just as he had predicted when he bolts awake to a blood red sunrise, his driver dutifully packing the jeep for another day on the road.

The heat is slow and baking and Calvin is continuously sleepy. He lolls in the steady, rhythmic jolting of the jeep's undulations and drinks from one of his cheap bottles of rum, spreading a milky sun block ointment over his pink face, a merciful remnant of a purchase made in Florida and the sole possession in his pocket when he left the bus. Calvin calculates that he has a week, possibly two weeks worth of supplies remaining.

The road is dull and featureless, the sun is relentless. Calvin catches the driver casting glances toward himself and the bottle of rum, but he tells himself that there is no way that he is going to share his liquor with this person. No fucking way. The man has to drive. Keep him sober. He casts his own furtive sidelong glances at the man, in whose hands, he has trusted his life. His very dependence on the driver in turn causes him no small resentment. What an unsavory dull sort of creature this is. But in the next moment he actually feels a stray spark of compassion, even pity. How complicated I am, Calvin thinks to himself.

Money changes hands every morning. Sometimes they argue, without understanding each other. The second night they camp in an isolated village off the road where Calvin is invited to spend the night in a crowded straw hovel filled with a smoky meat stench. He imagines that freshly dead bodies are buried beneath his mat. All night long he imagines and dreams of grasping hands coming towards him. Rapid voices speak on and on from dark corners of the hut. He steals himself outside where to his relief he finds his driver, sleeping on the ground, looking oddly peaceful. Calvin rousts him. They argue but Calvin pays a little extra and they are on their way. The road appears disappears and reappears ever appearing to lead them nowhere, the same dull, repetitive turns and straight-aways, the landscape tedious and exotic at the same time, like some distant planet, scrub and dust. At least once every other day, they are able to stop at identical looking villages where they are able to provision themselves with at least enough rice and water to continue the journey.

Calvin shares his food begrudgingly. They speak as little as possible. On more than one occasion they get stuck in a hole in the road or a tire blows flat. Through such urgencies they manage to cooperate enough to push together, or sometimes Calvin, to his chagrin, pushes by himself while the driver puts his foot on the gas. Fortunately, the jeep is not very big. Calvin is sure the driver must feel amused that Calvin must push his jeep, even spatter his already tattered clothing to exert himself, while he, the native driver, remains seated in the car. One day, perhaps, Calvin ruefully speculates, a tire will blow out completely into tiny shards and they will be utterly screwed and forced to hitchhike or else simply lay down and die.

One day, they slowly an overturned bus, much like the one he had once traveled on. Several young men sit upon the upended side of the vehicle, calmly smoking cigarettes. Bodies lay strewn and broken on either side and underneath. A skinny ox lies off the road, while two men, their heads and bodies covered in shredded rags kneel and seem to pray over its body. Calvin makes eye contact with one of the slit eyed youths who is smoking. Even at a distance, Calvin feels like he might fall inside that vacant stare. The driver yawns and they continue driving. Two days later they come across a similar accident at night, only there are no bodies nor any loitering survivor.

By the ninth day, Calvin has no idea that it is the ninth day. He exists in a state beyond boredom, utterly lost. Suddenly he thinks to himself that he is about to run out of money. He calculates he has just enough to pay for the driver to take him to the next village. Perhaps he will sell his passport. Their food is very low. But Calvin has barely eaten for two days. He is barely conscious for much of the time, the heat, the monotony, and the rum, all have worn him down. It occurs to him to be surprised that he can tolerate this featureless routine. Indeed, he realizes he must be attached to it.

By midday, they pull into a village that is uncannily familiar to him. Absolutely everything looks the same to him. There is the same green, skeletal looking gas pump, reserved for passing military personnel and government officials, but also, happily, available to anyone else with hard foreign currency, like American dollars. As he replaces the rusty pump, the driver smiles at Calvin. "Nous sommes presque la. Nous sommes presque a Chad," he lisps in his execrable French.

Suddenly Calvin is completely present to his strange surroundings. He tries to look at himself in the rear view mirrors but quickly sees that there aren't any. He knows though by touching himself that he is a chapped and crab like creature, red and mottled in his soiled K-Mart clothing, sitting squat beneath the African sun. He stares at his driver, whose name he cannot remember or never knew at all. Then with an energy that barely seems to be his own he flings himself upon the driver, managing to pin him briefly against the hood of the car.

"You lying son of a bitch!"

"Quoi?"

"You stupid bastard. You think I don't know what you're doing?"

"Eh....t'es fou, t'es fou, toi, mec!" You're crazy! You're crazy, man. Then the glistening bony matter of his jaw chatters and spews on and on in some guttural, stump of primitive tongue.

"Shut the fuck up! Look at this piece of shit we're in. You think I don't get it? This is the same goddamn village we sat down in

28

yesterday, the same one we were in a week ago, too, and every fucking day in between," Calvin screams, fleck and spittle spewing at the driver. "Where are the border guards, the police. You think I think we can just cross borders without getting shaken down by some punk with a rifle? You are driving us around in some crazy, pointless circle, around and around in this endless, pointless, empty parking lot while you bleed me dry!" he shouts. For a moment, he catches sight of the expanse of land beyond the road, an endless sweep of rivets and canyons, whispers and hints of far away ghostlike hands of haunting trees, and rows of low hulking mountains, crowned by rows of more distant, more powerful, dreadful mountains. "My god, what a spectacular shit hole this place is."

The driver surprises Calvin by shoving him away and though it wasn't so hard, Calvin's knees buckle and he spills gratefully to the ground. He hears the driver rattle on as if in the distance, as if he had no connection with this man, or with anything else. He squints up at the scarecrow frame who is gesticulating upward, sweeping his charred poker arm across the sky, as if that were the path they had already taken. Some corner of Calvin's cogent mind remains to glean that the man is pointing to the arc and path of the sun as if signs in the sky clearly proved their continued eastward progress toward the heartland of Chad. Either that, or the man was now invoking some celestial god or demon to come down and smite Calvin where he lay.

On his feet again, creaking, and not knowing how he managed to get up, Calvin stumbles against the rear grate of the dilapidated vehicle. "Where is my rum?" he barks.

"Rien plus," spits the driver, looking like a blurry faced monster. No more, he says.

"Yes, there's more, there's more alright. There's at least one more fucking bottle, goddamn you." And he starts to rifle through the half opened provisions. Then he pulls the tarp away from the driver's thin cache of possessions. The driver protests anew. Next to the dusty water supply, next to the khaki hookah pipe, Calvin finds a half empty remainder of rum. "Aha! You thieving son of a bitch." he says, grabbing the bottle and moving around the jeep. "I'm getting in. You're getting in. And you're going to drive me to Chad. All the way."

"Mais. Mais c'est a moi. C'est a moi, cela." It's mine. It's mine! The black man insists, meaning the bottle. "Donne. Donne!" Give it, he shouts.

"I ain't givin' it to you, because it's mine, for Chrissake. You goddamn well know it's mine. Now drive!" Calvin commands, seated now in the torn and gaping passenger seat. The man looks at him through slits for eyes, then softens and shrugs and slowly gets into the jeep. He mutters, "Il faut ce qu'on en a besoin." He has to have what he needs. They drive on. Calvin makes a point of drinking the last of the rum all that day, as if to flaunt the fact that it is his to drink, and with the smugness that somehow the effects will last longer if taken all at once. Even feeling sickish and bloated in his body, he remains at a comfortable distance from himself. He observes that he is in the jeep, but no longer of the jeep. Or maybe, he thinks, hooking a crooked corner of a smile, since I can no longer feel the jeep on my ass, perhaps I and the jeep are one! Calvin attempts a chuckle but manages only a burp that brings an acid bile to the back of his throat. His head jerks up and he looks at the glaring bone colored sky in surprise. Somehow the sight of it frightens and further sickens him and he realizes in dismay and resignation that his bowels have betrayed him already. He is tired. Very tired. And he gives into the impulse to lower his head upon his chin and to give way to a heavy, defeated kind of sleep. As with most dreams, the kind that most people forget, Calvin's are far from vivid at first, lacking coherent narrative. Instead, they merely form a series of mumbling monologues and ruminations, soothing and rhythmic, at first, becoming taxing and noisome, assuming familiar though not reassuring voices. The first voice he recognizes is of all people, his onetime chess partner though the man's name escaped him. The man says things like, "you know it's this way and not that way, but this shouldn't be the problem, it's just a matter of how you look at it, if you choose to look at it, which you might just as easily choose not to do, which is up to you. But in any case, it doesn't really matter unless you choose to make it matter in which case it matters to just that extent that you choose or not..." and so on. It occurs to Calvin that Joel isn't really talking to him, but is on his own journey of lostness, too. The Philipino ensign sits quietly to the side, nodding, observing sadly, his uniform newly whitened, stiffly starched, officers cap upon his head. So near and yet so far. Ernestia is the one person he expects to see and hopes he will, but she is nowhere to be found. Nothing but fake fruits and vegetables, computer screens, and words and words all jumbled together. Then he sees another car driving, driving, perhaps alongside his own, and it turns faster and faster, until suddenly it

30

smashes with an shrieking crash into something larger than itself, suddenly mangled in every way, just sitting there now, transformed. He moves closer to the ugly thing which no longer resembles a car. For a long time he stares at the strange wreck, steeped in sudden silence. The closer he approaches the smaller the terrible mangled thing appears, the more grotesque. A nose, a hand, a tiny finger peeks out. Body parts, bone and flesh compacted everywhere, all of it, insinuating, pathetic, accusatory. Revolted, Calvin opens his eyes, utterly surprised at first to look at the strange, jaundiced sky. Ah, I'm still dreaming then, he shrewdly surmises. It takes a moment for him to take it in, and he pulls himself up in his seat, sticky, sweaty, his lower back beginning to ache in a way that proves he has in fact awakened. Half expecting the jeep would actually have been overturned, as if he were the victim of the accident in his dream, it takes him a moment longer still to realize that the car is sitting still, silent at the side of the road, the landscape ever the same, perhaps yet more desolate, the air beginning to cool.

Stiffly turning his neck, he takes in that the driver is gone. For a long time, Calvin does nothing. Finally, he gets out of the vehicle, suspecting it is disabled. Indeed, he soon discovers the right rear tire has completely blown out. Gone. Just as he had once foreseen, he thinks, with grim satisfaction. Is the man walking to the nearest garage to look for a fresh tire? Not likely. Certainly, the driver must have hitched a ride on a bus that not infrequently traversed the highway. Calvin concludes that he had certainly been correct that they were in fact no more than a few miles from the town where they had met and first embarked and that he indeed had been slowly ripped off the entire time. He checks his pants and feels almost vindicated that his wallet and passport are gone, wondering at his utter lack of panic at his uncertain situation. He then begins a search of the entire vehicle, wondering if something may have been left behind. To his astonishment, he finds a lonely bottle of rum in the back. He grabs it and begins walking with renewed confidence in the direction that the car had previously been headed.

Clasping his miracle bottle as the afternoon cools, his feet seem to carry him with surprising lack of effort. It is not for me to think about which way I am headed, he tells himself, and he laughs at himself, keeping knowledge of his predicament at a safely remote distance from himself. Coolness, aloneness, and comfort await him. He turns behind him to his left, angry red scars pressing the horizon. The sky deepens and

31

the landscape grays. Soon it will be dark.

He feels vaguely excited and confident. After not too long he sees a pair of headlights appears in the distance, approaching slowly at first. A bus. Though a long ways off at first, disappearing and reappearing in the uneven road, suddenly he hears the engine rattle and groan as the bus bears down on him. Finally it slows and pulls alongside him. It hisses into park, the engine still growling. The driver leans out, a pair of bright frowning eyes piercing its way out of a jet black head, his arm resting where the driver's window would be if there had been a window. For a moment, they stare at each other.

The man gestures to Calvin, speaking rapidly and unintelligibly, nodding his head toward the passenger entrance. Calvin stares. Obviously he is being coaxed into entering the bus. Calvin smiles and asks the man in English, "Is this bus going to Chad?" The driver's frown deepens, his eyes narrow.

"Chad!" Calvin repeats.

To his surprise, the driver responds awkwardly, but in English. "What? You say Chad? *Chad?*"

"I'm going to Chad. The country, the republic of Chad" Calvin says proudly.

"Get in the bus," the driver commands. "I take to the village" he says, pointing in front of him.

"Oh? Is *that* the way to the land of Chad?" Calvin asks pointing back toward the broken down jeep, already knowing that the answer is certainly 'no'.

".......What?? Chad? You speak of Chad? No. No Chad. No Chad. I take to the village. Get in now."

"Well that's very nice of you, but you see I'm really headed only to the wonderful, enchanted land of Chad," Calvin insists.

"What? Get in the bus!" the driver says. "No more bus tonight. Get in!" Voices murmur in back of the driver. He turns and speaks loudly, urgently, in his wildly nonsensical native tongue. Then he turns back to Calvin and glaring, he leans out, and more worried than angry, he says, "Get in the bus." He points at Calvin. "You. Get in the bus. Or I leave. *No more bus!*"

Calvin breathes in and shrugs and says, "I appreciate that. And it's been very nice talking with you. Really. But you're just not going where I'm going. Really you aren't."

32

Again they stare at each other one last time, and the fierce look in the driver's eyes which once resembled anger now changes to fear. He pulls his head back, stares at the road, puts the bus in gear again. And drives away. Slowly. Inexorably.

Calvin happily watches the bus disappear. He thinks he can detect faces in the back pressed out of what used to be windows, staring at him, staring in wonder. Then he sees nothing but a single red tail light winking at him. Then nothing at all. Calvin turns and walks along the road, which is really just a rutted dirt path wide enough for a single vehicle. The sun has disappeared and suddenly the world is dark where he stands.

High above him, he begins to notice a marvel that somehow he had never previously grasped in all his days out here. The heavens exploding above him. So busy, yet remote and frozen, astonishingly bright. Calvin stoops at the sight, as if a cluster of stars were about to rain down at any moment on top of him. The violent vault of intrusive stars. He walks. Afraid, yet exhilarated. He clutches the bottle, partly to steady himself. Feels achy but moves on. Then he remembers that the sunset was behind him, off to his left. So he veers off the road, at first moving towards what he believed was where the sunset had been. A faint noise of reason reaches him, stops him, and he remembers. Sunset is west, sunrise is east. He turns again, stumbling, clutching his bottle, not quite sure of his direction. It takes longer than he might have expected to reach the road again.

A faint wind rises, touching him it feels from a distant and unearthly place. He looks up then away, the sight of the sky inducing the suggestion of nausea. Calvin walks on. The light from the sky, even with no moon is still light enough for him to see the ground in front of him, yet not quite light enough to chase away strange distortions. Objects that must surely be quite small, rocks and low lying brush, seem to hulk in wait to ensnare him. He takes small steps, walking away from the road, walking toward the east, walking towards Chad. The sound of his feet crunching the earth seems unexpectedly loud. He remembers - of all things - the stirring of a fork in the sink of his apartment. Somehow it must have been placed on top of something else, and something displaced it, water dripping or draining, and then the fork simply ....moved. Just a bit. Made a sound, a small sound. That was it. Nothing more. Calvin stops for a moment in the hulking darkness,

33

daring to look upward, feeling the lifting wind, wind that came from the stars themselves. And he marvels at the insignificance, the inconsequence of his memory, the memory that impresses upon him, the fork in the sink. What about this fork? Nothing. And yet, Calvin decides, unable to suppress a smile, this memory, this infinitesimal event, this was the key. Surely this was the key to everything. Everything! Elated, he declares that this indeed was the single most important thing that had ever happened to him, hearing the fork settle in his sink. It was surely the symbol and nexus of his entire life. He laughs out loud, or at least he thought he had, for no sound comes forth. Only the wind. Thank you, he wanted to say. Thank you for revealing to me my life's worth, my life's meaning. Thank you. Thank you!

Onward.

Suddenly the earth sinks away from him and he finds himself slipping, slipping, falling, and clutching the bottle as if clutching solid earth. He continues to skid and slide, feeling the icy scrape of the earth cut into his legs, rocks needling and grinding into his back. Finally, he stops moving and all is silent.

For a long moment he lays perfectly still, his entire body throbbing. He tries to divine what has happened, where he is, whether it is safe to sit up or to move at all. Yes the bottle was is still there, still intact. Ah yes. He gingerly casts about his limbs seeking information. The earth is soft and moist here. His left foot is shoeless. Even more interesting it hangs in the air. After a time, Calvin discerns that he has slid, not just down a ditch, but indeed down the shallow part of a canyon wall towards a ledge, inches perhaps from being jettisoned off a ninety degree cliff. He feels about for a pebble and carefully tosses it. And waits. One one thousand two one thousand three one thousand four one thousand..... then a distant echoing plink. His gut sickens but at least he knows he is correct in his surmise.

His remaining goal is to put himself into as comfortable a sitting position as possible. Fortunately, the ledge is wide enough for him to rest his weight upon it while still leaning back against the earth. From this position, though unable to divine anything about the world below, he retains an unobstructed view of outer space, or at least the eastern sky.

For a long time he thinks of nothing, even forgetting his bottle. Suddenly remembering it, he opens it and drinks from it as if slowly, passionately embracing a beautiful woman. No hunger, no cold,

34

somehow. Sheltered for the most part from the wind. A little pain and discomfort, nothing to worry about. Nothing to pay attention to.

Feeling clear in his head, he considers how very lucky he is. I could have cracked my skull. I could have cracked the bottle! Here I am, facing eastward. Facing Chad! And again, he opens his mouth to laugh out loud, but only the wind comes out.

He dares to contemplate the angry torrent of distant stars, trying to compare it to his precious fork in the sink. Briefly he remembers his dream and the car crash at the motel. He must surely name a constellation after it, for the wreckage is everywhere, crushed across the sky. It is the fork though that wins out in his memory, though the car crash tries to menace him from the heavens. Remember the fork. Only the fork! The fork is all! The fork encompasses and embraces all. Again, he takes a drink. Just take a little. Just enough for now.

Who else will come to join him in his invitation to memory? Who else will challenge the fork settling in his sink? His mother? His father? Ernestia? He invites Ernestia to come join him on the ledge. For a moment. Only for a moment. But no. Why bother. The fork. Only the fork, he thinks proudly. Once more, he tries unsuccessfully to laugh.

One more swig? Just for now. Then. Silence.

He smiles, no longer frightened of the sky. Though his heart beats mightily, he smiles. Just the sky, the bottle, his heart beat. Silence. He holds the bottle closer to him, anxious only that it's less than two thirds full now. Still. More than half full. More than half to go. I can be patient. I can make that last a while longer, he thinks, suppressing his thirst, relishing the heat of his face, his ears tingling from the alcohol inside him. His stomach suddenly winces and twists, but he ignores that.

Still more silence. Then the wind to keep him company again.

He wishes only that his bottle might last forever. And the night itself. And the wind. This is all he wants. He grins and asks - finally aloud, his voice faint but distinctly his own - 'Is that really too much to ask?'

A FITTING CONCLUSION TO A SUCCESSFUL EVENING

Two men emerge from the hotel. Ralph is tall and pear shaped. Jacob Marx is short and fat, sturdy and balding with glasses.

Ralph hopes and believes that he has acquitted himself at least fairly well tonight at the trade show. Naturally it was Jacob Marx who really owned the crowd. That's good, though. You're not supposed to outshine your boss. The only thing, Ralph recalls is that he nearly tripped over the microphone cord after being introduced as the product line coordinator. To cover up his stumble, he pretended to jog a few steps, as if he had intended to make this spritely move all along. Ralph decides to mention this later so that they might share a good laugh about it. Maybe Jacob Marx will even thank Ralph for such quick thinking and such self-deprecating humor that suggests a much deeper self-confidence.

Instead of heading for their cars, the two men decide to walk four blocks to a pizza parlor. This decision happily presents still further opportunities for Ralph to connect with his boss. They arrive, make their purchases and begin to walk back, eating along the way, the tall man gesticulate, the short man chewing vigorously. I'll tell him one more time how successful the event was, or better still, perhaps tie in one of the themes from his speech into my idea for the new product line.

Drifting slowly ahead is a man in a tired, suit, shiny with wear, with only a yellowed T-shirt beneath, tennis shoes, and a sunburnt face. Ralph looks up and the man mumbles his plea in a voice too easily ignored. He pats his pant pocket as if looking for change but in the next sliver of a second they have already passed the man as irrevocably as if he had never existed.

They fall into silence. Ralph turns to his boss with an apologetic smile. "I feel bad sometimes when they ask for money."

"Who?"

"That homeless guy."

"Oh. Well, you didn't see *me* pretend to reach for my pocket book." And Jacob Marx gives him a wink.

"Oh. You didn't see him."

"Of course I saw him. He's looking for his next fix or his next drink out of a brown paper bag. I guarantee it."

Ralph's mind flashes upon the literal worthlessness of his boss' "guarantee". He imagines winking back at his boss. Instead, he smiles, knowingly. "Yeah, I know. But there's also a lot of people who can't find work."

"Yes. There are."

"I feel lucky that I have a job," Ralph says, throwing Jacob Marx a sideling glance.

"And well you should," the man says tossing yet another wink at Ralph. "I used to think that these guys were just hungry. They probably are, too. They should be, I guess. I mean everyone has to eat. I see them all the time downtown. I'm not a stone, you know. So whenever I happen to have food with me, I offer it to them, like if I have an extra sandwich or something."

"You carry extra sandwiches with you?"

"My point is this," and he stops and faces Ralph, "not once has any guy I've offered food to ever accepted. It makes you wonder."

"I think I see your point."

They continue walking down the empty street. Ralph speaks, "I mean, don't you think some of these guys are mentally ill or don't have family?"

"What's that got to do with anything? Even if they're mentally ill, they still know they need to eat. So why would they refuse food from someone they had just solicited, unless what they really want is something else entirely. Make sense?"

"Yes."

"Sometimes I try to give them a sandwich still in its wrapping. A perfectly good tuna fish sandwich. They don't want it. I'm telling you. So I give money instead to shelters and well vetted community centers. I strongly advise you to do the same. That's what does a lot of good. And that's what you want to do too, I guarantee it."

"Give to community centers?"

"Do some good is what I meant, but yes. I can recommend some places. I think I'm paying you enough so you can afford it, since you seem to feel bad about it. Good for you, by the way. For caring."

Ralph is stunned to hear himself ask his boss, "Are you saying you used to buy extra sandwiches and carry them with you in case a homeless person approaches you?"

"I think you're missing the point, which I have known you to do, young man."

"Sorry."

"Believe it or not, I've survived some hard times myself," and so Jacob Marx begins to share his own narrative; on his own from the age of seventeen, working his way through school in crappy jobs, married at nineteen, his first son born before he turned twenty-one, his parents in ill health. It seems to Ralph as if Jacob Marx is presenting his story as if he expects it to be received with appreciation, an approximation of intimate sharing, yet Jacob Marx himself is far away as he tells the tale that he has told before.

"I forget. Are you married?"

"No sir. I had a girl-friend a few months ago. For a little while. Things were going great when--"

"Children?" Jacob Marx interrupts

"Oh no."

"That's fine. Do things in the right order. Don't do things like I did," and Jacob Marx winks yet again, an ironical wink, since after all, he, Jacob Marx, after first living a life full of precocious and intimidating responsibility, nevertheless triumphed in life, a highly respected and successful business man, all three children grown, married or in college,. Or maybe it's just a wink and a wink means nothing at all.

Ralph smiles because he thinks he is supposed to smile and a moment later he asks his boss, "I did OK tonight, didn't I?"

Jacob Marx does not answer at first. "Yes. Fine." Good. "Yes. You did fine. I know you know your material. I just want to make sure that everyone else sees what we see. I think you could have helped me tell a more compelling story with the market data."

"Oh. Really?"

"Yes. Really. We need to excite our sales force. I think I compensated for this so we're good. But it's not always going to be me out front. I can't be everywhere."

"Yes, but I hope I at least showed how we can penetrate the market through key segmentation within our core demographics ----"

"I want them to see dollars. I want them to see their future. Our future. And I want to see you - Ralph Henderson – to be more assertive. When you get in front of our sales force, I want you to be bold; I want you to tell a compelling story with the data – not just data for data's sake - one that our sales force can really relate to. And maybe put in some more pie charts and colors, too. Not too many, though. Just enough."

Ralph responds in a retreating voice that might have been intended only for himself, "I did use the data, all of the data to show where we are projected to –"

"Oh, and you tripped on the microphone cord when you came up on stage."

"I know. I tried to pull it off like I meant to step like that all along."

"I thought you were going to stumble into me and knock me on my ass, young man," and he pushes out a hard born chuckle. "I guess you can get through a lot of things if you can laugh at yourself. Make sense?"

Ralph opens his mouth to speak, nothing coming forth, when another homeless man appears, seemingly from nowhere, a ragged black man of wiry build with coiling dreadlocks, young but wizened, wearing a button-less vest and bell bottoms. He calls out to them, "Hey, can either or both of you nice businessmen spare me a dollar so I can get me something to eat tonight?" The man pushes the word, *eat*. The two men pass but the man with dreadlocks falls easily in step with them. "I'm hungry... And I'm askin' you nicely."

"No money. But you want a piece of my pizza?" Jacob Marx asks without looking up, gesturing to the small pizza box in his right hand. The homeless man grunts, surprised, considering the offer. "Come on over," Jacob Marx says in a booming, affable voice, eyes still fixed straight ahead. Then he says, "we'll have it at my house."

Both of them continue walking while the stranger jolts to a sudden stop. Ralph does not turn to see his face, nor does he want to, but flushed in his own face, he continues walking straighter and faster toward the parking lot. The voice quickly catches up with them. "Aw man, cut the bullshit. What the fuck you talkin' about? You think you funny?" They keep walking. "Maybe I *will* come over. See how you like *that*."

Ralph cringes. How could his boss not realize what he was saying, to whom he was saying it, and where? Could Jacob Marx have actually thought he was being *funny?* The man with the dreadlocks continues to follow, no longer interested in money or pizza.

"Hey! You! Don't *insult* me man. That ain't right. Maybe I need money to eat but you still have to treat me with *some* respect!" he says, gathering his dignity into a weapon.

"I withdraw the remark," says Jacob Marx. "It's like I never said it."

"You what?" The man's voice inflects in falsetto.

"You heard me."

"You seriously gonna pretend you said nothing? Look, I ain't playin' no game here. I'm just trying to get something to eat. You understand me?"

They come to a stop light that has turned red. No cars in front, only the man with the dreadlocks unseen behind them. They all stand still and straight, obeying the traffic light. The homeless man curses softly to himself, his outrage perhaps having peaked. Ralph, neck hairs raised, furtively looks behind to see what the other man is doing. The man has settled in front of a darkened restaurant at the corner, shifting his weight, hands in his pockets, muttering, head down, soothing himself. Suddenly he looks at Ralph and at the very moment that eye contact is made, Ralph finds it impossible to break it, so that he now finds himself actually staring at the man.

"What *you* lookin' at now?"

"I'm sorry," Ralph hears himself say, "I..."

The boss breaks in, "Ralph, it would be better if we just left. Don't say anything."

The homeless man asks, "Are you his daddy? Is he your daddy?" the man says turning to Ralph.

"No, I'm not his daddy. Do we look alike?" Jacob Marx answers evenly, "You want to adopt him?" Clearing thorns from his thoughts, Ralph reasons that Jacob Marx thinks he can control the situation with levity, that he still owns the stage, that he can still create the illusion that they share their circumstances as one big joke, all three of them.

40

The man addresses Ralph. "He ain't your daddy. Why you listen to this fat ass bag-a-bullshit?"

"What?"

"Big bag a bullshit, I said."

The man has just called Jacob Marx a "fat-ass", a "bag-a-bullshit". Ralph accepts these insults as literal descriptions, revealing Jacob Marx as nothing more than a great swollen bag bursting with excrement. Nor can Ralph push away another image more unacceptable still, of his boss's own buttocks, sweaty, hirsute, magnified by pimples and moles, nubby and blistering, seated heavily upon the toilet, flapping blow noises, grunting, anus discharging heavily the bullshit, salvo after salvo, into the bowl, water splashing, more gushing out.

"Look," Ralph hears himself say, feeling nauseous. "We didn't mean anything. We didn't mean to insult you."

"Thank you Ralph, I can speak for myself."

"Why don't you let this man talk?" asks the dreadlocks man. "You just talk shit. Your mouth move and your lips flippity-flap but you don't say nothin' do you?"

"I've got nothing to say to you," Jacob Marx says, as if making the man's point.

"Where your house at? We all goin' over and eat *pizza* now?" he asks, articulating the word pizza with a big slapstick emphasis as if pizza were the most comical yet insulting thing imaginable. Ralph suppresses a snigger like a muffled sneeze. They walk in step like old friends, the man with the dreadlocks almost walking between them, close enough to link arms, looking to any onlookers as if he were there to cheer up his dour companions.

"Look," Jacob Marx speaks again, looking straight ahead, away from the man, "I already told you. I withdraw my invitation. We've all been feeling a little tired tonight. Perhaps another time, sir."

"Where you live man?"

"None of your business!"

"Where you live?"

"Goodnight and goodbye!"

"Where you *live?*"

They had nearly reached the garage. Ralph looks inside longingly as if the parking structure were a safe haven where this man would somehow not be able to follow. "This conversation is now over," says Jacob Marx.

"Ain't nothin' over yet, fat ass. Where you live now? Beverly Hills?"

"Over."

"Bel Air? Rancho Park? *Trous*dale?"

Ralph has had enough. Of both of them. As if reading his thoughts, the man suddenly addresses him. "Hey, where *you* live?"

"What?"

"You heard me. Where you live? Where he live?"

"Don't you make me part of this!" Ralph says with a vehemence that doesn't even feel like it's his own.

Jacob Marx looks at him. The homeless man says, "How you not part of this? You part a him, aintcha?"

"None of your goddamn business," Ralph hisses through clenched teeth.

The man with the dreadlocks pauses for a long second. "Oooh! Is that right? So you all tough now, ain't you." He turns back to Jacob Marx. "You know where I live don't you? Right? That ain't no secret. You know where I live. You want to guess? You want to guess where I live?"

"Get away from us," Ralph growls.

The man smiles. "You all just lucky, tough boy. You lucky I don't feel like goin' to jail tonight." What Ralph needed to defend just at that moment, he would never quite know; maybe his right to exist. He had often fantasized about situations like this one, full of danger, yet there was always a loved one, maybe his mother, or better still some as yet unknown tender innocent thing that needed his protection. Did Jacob Marx need or deserve the same protection?

Ralph mutters as if to himself yet perfectly out loud, "You're lucky you don't feel like getting your head split open tonight," and the man with the dreadlocks hears every word.

"Excuse me?"

"Nothing."

"You wanna split my head open?"

"Nothing!" Ralph's stomach sours and tightens as his heart rate drives further up.

42

"What are you doing Ralph?" Jacob Marx says. "This guy just wants to bullshit. Let's not provoke the situation. Let's go."

"This man just wants something to eat and just a little tiny bit of respect. That's what this man wants. Ain't you been listening to a word I been saying? Hell no."

"You still want this pizza? It's yours!" says Jacob Marx.

The man eyes the box for a moment. He looks up cautiously at Jacob Marx's face. He narrows his eyes at what he sees; the narrowest hint of a smile. "Get that fuckin' nasty thing away from me. I don't need your half eaten pizza."

"Just like I told you, Ralph," says Jacob Marx.

"What'd you tell him?" asks the homeless man.

"None of your business."

"You tell him that I wouldn't accept your ratty half eaten pizza. That I just want a dollar to go get high in the sky. That's what you told him. Right?"

Ralph speaks. "He said, none of your goddamn business!"

"And what do you say. You say you wanna split my head open?"

"I'm saying nothing." Ralph says dismissively, feeling himself turn red, waving his hand as if it were something else entirely that he is being mistaken for.

"What that mean? You pleadin' the fifth. Nothin'. Head splittin' ain't nothing."

"I didn't say that."

"Yeah you did. Don't back away from your word. I heard you say you wanna split my head open."

"Yeah you said it, Ralph," says Jacob Marx. "But he didn't mean it. OK? Nobody means anything they are saying right now, OK?"

Ralph briefly turns to his boss, astonished. Then he faces the homeless man again. "Look. You threatened us first. You..... Look, I said, 'You're lucky you *don't* want your head split open." What does that even mean Ralph thinks to himself, his throat feeling small and dry.

"Jesus, Ralph. Enough already," says his boss.

"Well I'm *standing* right here," says the man "Here's my head. You see my head? You ready to do some splittin' here? Hungry black man wants a dollar to eat so you ready to split his head? You ready?"

"Go away!"

The man laughs and slips his hand into his pant pocket, looking like he is gripping something. "Come on. Make your move Mr. Head Splittin' motherfucker. Let's see what you got. It's your move. I'm waitin.'"

"I'm not makin' any damned move."

"Fine," says Jacob Marx

"Look," says Ralph. "I didn't say that. What I meant is that if you *do* want your head," Ralph says, his face burning and sweat searing beneath his scalp. "if you want it...split open.... Ah Jesus, what the fu--- , anyway, if that's what you want, then you make your goddamn move."

"Oh for God's *sakes!*" mutters Jacob Marx. But the two men have no more need for him. The homeless man stares, his nostrils flare, head moving slightly, their eyes locked. Ralph eyes the man's hand. Knife? Gun? His heat pounds behind his teeth.

Jacob Marx breaks in one last time. "Tell you what. How about no one goes to jail tonight and no one gets their head split open, gentlemen. Sound fair?" Jacob Marx's attempt at diplomacy goes unheard for he no longer exists. Ralph looks into the homeless man's yellowed, cue-ball eyes. He feels his own pupils dilate. It is the man with the dreadlocks who blinks, whose shiny yellows gleam just the slightest sliver of surprise, for he now looks up at Ralph who is the much bigger man.

"You in *my* house now," the man says, without much conviction, and he pulls up his hand out of his pocket. Ralph's insides flame and he steps on the man's foot, raises his left hand as if to push him and flings his right fist toward the other's head. The punch barely glances off the side of the man's forehead. Ralph hits him again, this time with no force, limp fist, as in slow motion. The man's eyes glower. Ralph hits him a third time in quick succession; disgusted with himself and frightened for having missed before, this time Ralph throws his fist shoulder length from his legs and it lands, sinking into the center of the other's face with a fury that seems to belong to someone else from far away. The homeless man's head snaps back, hands raised as if in serene protest, please kindly wait until I am ready. In a sluggish corner of his mind, it occurs to Ralph, you've hit him three times, no fair. Yet he draws forward to hit him again. The arm from underneath the bent head of the homeless man swings out like a tennis back hand and Ralph feels a sharp sensation trace across his chest. You ripped my shirt! Just then he falls

44

with all his weight upon the collapsing man below. They grope upon the pavement. Pin pricks shoot up Ralph's upper back and as their eyes lock, he furiously grabs the man's right arm and twists it to the ground driving his own knee upon the neck of the man, slicing his own palm as he grabs for the knife, a sickening burn, and blood squeezing through his clenched fingers. He seizes the man's wrist, both hands now, inefficiently twisting the wrist to wrench away the knife, when suddenly there is a great impact as if something had smashed up from beneath the sidewalk; Jacob Marx's boot thudding into the homeless man's ear. The man holds fast to the knife so Jacob Marx kicks him again. Harder. As the boss kicks him a third time, Ralph suddenly sees the hand more clearly, coldly examines where to apply pressure and with a single wrench sends the knife skidding across the pavement. So he pins the man to the ground and all fight seems to drain from him.

Jacob Marx curses to himself and looks at his shoes, as if irritated at scuffing them. Ralph looks up, "Don't kick him anymore!"

"Is he conscious?"

"Yeah," Ralph answers breathing heavily, nose running all of a sudden. "Yeah I think so."

"Son of a bitch. Are you all right?" Jacob Marx asks, "You're bleeding." They look at each other a moment, Ralph with his shirt shredded, blood already clotting on his upper chest and back and running slowly from his left palm and across his sleeve.

"Get an ambulance," Ralph says. They speak to each other as if the homeless man no longer exists.

"Lemme go," hisses the man, weakly.

Jacob Marx's face darkens. "I really think we have to make sure this bastard is incapacitated."

"And do *what*?"

"He stabbed you."

"Get an ambulance," Ralph repeats.

"Should we...Can you keep him down while I make the call?" asks the boss man.

The homeless man lies still. "Yeah, sure," Ralph replies. "Just get the knife before you go." He notices some stray on-lookers from across the street.

"I'll handle it so there aren't any finger prints," says Jacob Marx, as if he were in a police movie.

"Why? There all his, not mine."

"I mean I don't want to add my own." And he takes out a soiled handkerchief and carefully scoops up the knife. Then he strides off to find the nearest phone, eyeballs wary, weaving. Ralph looks down reluctantly at the man. Now they can talk. The man leans away coughing, an absurdly polite looking gesture.

"Why did you have to act so stupid?" Ralph says to him. As if in reply, the man hawks up a bloody gob of green phlegm upon the sidewalk and continues coughing. His left ear is still swollen and glistening. "Sorry about your ear. I'm sorry. I'm sorry! I'd like to let you go. Look, I was the one who wanted to apologize. Remember? I wanted to apologize! I wanted to apologize." Ralph says, mustering a thin protective coat of anger.

The homeless man doesn't look up. He closes his eyes slightly. Finally he says in a faded voice, "Just get off me. Mr. Head Splitter Apology Fool." He seems strangely calm. Ralph looks up and sees three men walking towards him. One is black, about forty with a growth of facial stubble, wearing a blue work shirt open over a T-shirt. The other men are younger. The blue shirt man looks gravely at Ralph who is frozen absurdly on top of the homeless man.

"What the hell are you doing?" says blue shirt man, with surprising mildness.

"This guy picked a fight with us," Ralph explains. He sounds whiny to his own ears. "He pulled a knife on me. Look!" he says, nodding to where there is blood on his shirt. The blue shirt man slowly shakes his head.

"He attacked me!" the homeless man suddenly shouts. "He hit me three times. I never hit him. He told me he split my head open. *I* was the one acting in self-defense. It was me. Not you, you pansy fat ass."

Ralph tightens his grip on the man, angry to have been labeled with the same insult as his boss. "You followed us. You threatened us," he answers, but he feels bored saying so.

"Who's *us*?" blue shirt man asks, "You gotta friend?"

"There are two of us," Ralph blandly answers.

"I see. And this man here threatened the *two* of you?"

"Get off me!"

"Where's your friend?" asks blue shirt man.

46

"He's not my friend. But he went to call an ambulance."

"You through beating this man up?"

"Yes," Ralph answers, respecting the other's presumed authority. He detects reasonableness there. "I guess he's through stabbing me" Ralph adds.

"I don't see a knife in his hand. Get off him."

"We're waiting for the ambulance."

"Well he don't need you sitting on top of him like that, puttin' more hurt on him. Get off of him. Now."

"Who are you?" Ralph asks.

"Never mind, just pick yourself up off his ass. He's not doin' nothing, I'm telling you."

"You're gonna take care of him?" Ralph asks.

"Will you just--come on," Ralph braces for a blow but instead the man picks him up and Ralph's hands just let go. He finds himself sitting with a thud on the pavement, a stiffness followed by a sharp pain shooting across his chest. Blue-shirt man kneels next to the man with the dreadlocks. "You're just lucky you look as bad as he do." Enough with people being lucky. "*Hey*, what the fuck happened to his damn ear?"

"The other guy did that." Ralph looks at the mangled ear shrinking with shame. Blue shirt man squats by the other who begins to lean up on his elbows and his palms. Ralph sits, creaky and stiff, palms burning. He vomits and wipes his mouth with the back of his hand. Trembling, he holds his palms together to staunch the bleeding. He wants to convey concern and smallness, rectitude. He has no idea whether these other men will beat him or help him or ignore him. Do the two black men know each other? Ralph wonders.

More people gather but everyone just seems to ignore him. He feels cold and sticky. After a short time he sees the marmalade light of the paramedics and the bright headlights of what must be a police car. Only then does he recognize Jacob Marx talking with a paramedic, standing oddly equal and comfortable next to the man with the blue shirt. Were they talking to each other? A light flickers in Ralph's face and a hand gently touches his shoulder and a voice he has never heard before addresses him.

"Are you Mr. Ralph Henderson?" Yes, he nods. "Were you involved in the altercation that took place in front of this parking structure about a half hour ago?" Yes, I was. The question is inane but polite. "Are you in any pain Mr. Henderson?" No, not really. A little. "We want you to let us lower you on your back." A patient neutral voice advises Ralph on exactly what the owner of that voice is going to do, where he is going to touch him and why. Every so often Ralph realizes that he is nodding. He feels his shirt being unbuttoned and he feels modest, embarrassed about his paunch.

"How are you doing young man?" Yes. *That* voice.

"Fine," he answers in a hoarse whisper, not looking up.

"Anything I can do?" Jacob Marx asks the paramedic who is kneeling over Ralph. So you're a doctor now as well, Ralph thinks and he almost laughs, but it feels like it might burn to do so.

The paramedic does not look up as he answers, "Mr. Henderson has received superficial lacerations, nothing major. We still want to patch him up and do the usual testing."

Ralph stares at the curbside as if it is not himself that lies upon it. It is as if there is no reason for him to be here or anywhere at all in particular. The next thing he knows, a police officer, faceless in the background glare of lights, begins to speak. "Mr. Henderson, we have a witness that tells us that you were assaulted tonight by a man wielding a switchblade."

"I was?"

"You're still bleeding a little."

"I guess I am. I'm sorry."

"Mr. Henderson, do you wish to press charges against the man who assaulted you?"

Ralph looks towards the cop, though not directly at him. The question presents itself to him as exceedingly nuanced and complex. He blinks and shrugs his shoulders. Something about the street at that moment, the bright lights from the garage and the emergency vehicles and the excess of people milling and talking, something about it feels perversely comforting to him, though impossibly distant. Suddenly he thinks he sees the homeless man being put into the ambulance, a bandage and compress on his ear. "I hope he's OK," Ralph says, but no one seems to hear him.

π

Jacob Marx comes and sits beside Ralph while he lies in bed at the emergency room, waiting to be discharged. "How are you, young man?"

Ralph gives him an incredulous look. "I don't know."

"You've been through a lot."

"Is he here?"

"Who? You mean *him*?"

"Yes."

"Maybe. But don't worry about him. You're not gonna see him."

"I'm not *worried*." Ralph says, and he winces at an unexpected shooting pain.

"Take it easy." They sit in silence for a moment, quiet amidst the bustle of the ER. Jacob Marx asks, "Do you feel well enough for me to ask you something?"

"I guess."

Jacob Marx leans forward. "What happened out there, Ralph?" There's a trace of a smile in his face.

"You saw what happened."

"You hit him."

"He had a knife."

"Exactly. You're lucky he didn't seriously injure you."

"Yes, lucky. But it was too late. He wasn't going to let it go."

"I guess you're sure about that."

"I'm sure." But in his own mind, Ralph isn't sure of anything, except that he resents the man before him for the story he has to tell. "If we had run, one of us would have been stabbed. Maybe you." Fatass, he thinks.

Jacob Marx leans back. "I think you might be right, young man. It was a bad situation and you handled it, Ralph."

Ralph stares at the ceiling for a long moment. "No I didn't"

"Sure you did. The whole thing was a gigantic ball of bullshit from the beginning."

"Yes. Yes, it was."

49

"But you handled it."

"You think so?"

"You just said there was no backing down. He was never going to leave it alone. He had a knife. There's no telling what he was going to do. So you handled it."

Ralph looks up at Jacob Marx, but he fails to meet his eyes. "No….I didn't," Ralph tells him, less because he knows this is true, for he has no idea what is still true, but rather because he feels he can say such a thing at this exact moment without bother of contradiction. He weeps. But only for a moment, as if someone else is weeping for him.

"It's OK," says Jacob Marx. "It's going to be OK." Ralph ceases his weeping at once. Jacob Marx smiles in recognition. A relentless surge of fury swells within Ralph and has nowhere else to go.

The man with the dreadlocks appears to him daily in fantasies and dreams for weeks, less frequently for months after that, and after more than two years only every once in a while. When he does reflect on that night he usually still longs to be approved, like a small child, and he imagines connecting with the homeless man through their shared wounds, with the aid of the man with the blue shirt. If there's still no approval….then he'll destroy the man! Because he has to. Then again at other times he simply nods and walks away with his dignity. Sometimes they agree to replay the whole street scene only this time Ralph openly rebukes his boss and gives the man the money. A bribe? No, not a bribe! Sometimes the homeless man just sniggers for Ralph's wounds are not worthy enough. You haven't suffered enough. Not nearly. Not unless you inflict a whole lot more pain on yourself, or else let me do it for you. *No*, that's bullshit too. He was simply defending himself. Wasn't he?

Then one night after two years he begins to dream that he and the man with the dreadlocks are laughing together, making each other laugh even more so whenever either of them says the words "head splitting". They are like actors in a movie who keep blowing their lines and descend into laughter together in outtake after outtake. And Jacob Marx cannot stand this because he cannot share in their hilarity. Ralph awakens and feels sad and disappointed in the man, as if the homeless man had been a friend, a friend who had let him down.

50

One day while leaving a record store in Westwood, Ralph sees the man again at last, still wearing the same bell bottoms, the same vest. It's him. It's really him! But he isn't panhandling; he is simply talking with another black man on the street. The ear looks completely healed but he can't tell for sure. Ralph imagines he has seen his old friend with whom he has had a most unfortunate quarrel and therefore they are now impossibly distant from one another. His heart pounds with the notion of amends, but of what sort and how? He watches for a long time, eager yet anxious. The man with the dreadlocks leaves while the other man remains. And in a flash Ralph is there watching himself earnestly pressing two $10 bills into the other's hand entreating him to give one to his friend. At first the other man raises his eyebrow and stares at Ralph as though he were a foolish person. But Ralph keeps talking and eventually the man presents a face of great solemnity and so Ralph believes that the homeless man will get the money, but he never knows for sure. He tells himself that the homeless man would likely have never been able to accept the money directly from him anyway, so it is better that he pass it on through his friend. No, it's not a bribe, he imagines telling the homeless man. It's a gift. It's a token, a symbol. No, not even that. It's simply a sign of respect. Or not even that. It's just starting over. As it should have been in the first place. With interest. It *must* be! Later that night he finds himself feeling utterly dissatisfied and the same familiar fury revisits with him with nowhere else to go.

One day, Ralph simply thinks of the incident no more and he prospers at his job. He even meets a fine sensible young woman and it seems like they will one day be married. Occasionally, he sees the homeless man in his dreams. He sees the man with the dreadlocks in the faces of other homeless men as well and he feels in their stare that they know, but in the next instant they are merely faces once more. Ralph works hard and he earns at last the increasing approval of his boss, and of all his many superiors, feeling frustrated only by an endless multitude of little things, with only occasional mild indigestion from too much work, food, or alcohol. He feels occasional stiffness and numbness in his left palm, and an infrequent visitation of that flat red fury that seems like it will never leave him until it finally does. Now and then it visits him even when his lady friend is cross or disappointed with him or talking

51

too endlessly about what he should do and what they should do.   But at least he feels no more shooting pains in his upper chest and back.

No more shooting pains.

WITH A FLICK OF THE WRIST

Jared never knew where all these impulses came from. He barely noticed them at all until one of them one day simply demanded to be noticed. Yet they came all the time; touch this, grab that, talk to that girl over there, jump fully clothed into the water, walk nude down the street, step off the curb in front of a speeding bus, kiss Isabelle. Of course, he never followed any of them at all. No, I will not do that, could never do that, he thought, even though at least some of them might be so easy, at least in principle. Just a quick motion. Of course, not all impulses, or were they desires, were meant to be weighted equally. Stepping off a curb is a simple thing, but stepping in front of a rushing bus is no joke at all. There were many things like that, Jared wondered, little steps you could take from which you could never return the same, if at all. He wondered, at times, whether you could measure how real you were by doing something outrageous, whether you could truly feel alive by stepping out in front of a speeding bus.

He and Albert were at the office, sitting in the kitchen. Albert spoke loudly, busying himself with the plastic wrapping of his tuna fish sandwich. They often had lunch together. Albert, the lady-killer salesman, and Jared, the inventory clerk. "I was really on a roll. Sometimes I had up to five or six people at my booth asking me questions. If one person asked, I'd answer the question for everyone, draw everybody in, it was great, I mean, I really had my act down." Jared wondered if Albert was really interested in his tuna fish. Albert had just returned from a convention, delighted to stand behind a linen draped table in a hotel ballroom, discussing office automation, trading business cards, glad-handing, winking. Jared smiled, noted the budding gleam in his colleague's eye, anticipating a tale about some gorgeous, well-healed babe he picked up over there.

"You're gonna die when you hear this, Jer". Albert called him Jerry. Jared objected. They settled on Jer. "I can't believe I did this.

53

This guy walks up to my table all casual, no suit. He's a midget; no, he's a dwarf, big head and all, short little body. And I'm so fired up greeting everyone that I just give him a loud hello and say, Good afternoon, what can I do for you, little fellow?"

"Little fellow?" Jared echoed with growing astonishment.

"No shit," Albert confirmed finally taking a bite of his sandwich, nodding furiously, smirking.

"You called someone 'little fellow' while working the booth? Jesus!" Jared exclaimed. "What were you thinking, Al?"

"That's just it. I wasn't. I was just going off. I was all pumped up, talking to everyone in sight. My mouth just...flies ahead of my brain, I guess. Can you believe that? Man, did I bust myself." Jared admired this combination of honesty and shamelessness. Al just screwed up. Wasn't life a big learning experience? Why be unhappy?

"So what happened? Did...did you talk after that?"

"Yeah! He told me about his office set-up and everything. Never really looked me in the eye though. Not that he could have, you know. Ha! I don't think he was really a serious buyer, anyway. A bullshitter."

"The little fellow was a bullshitter?"

"Hey Jer, so what's the deal with this French chick? You goin' out again?"

"Isabelle?" Ah, Isabelle. Eez-a-bell. "Yeah. We've been out twice already. I really like her....No Al, nothing's happened yet," anticipating Albert's obvious question, annoyed.

"No? You sure she doesn't have a boyfriend somewhere?"

Jared shrugged, "No. I don't think she does. I don't know. Maybe."

"It's your move, buddy boy. She's waiting for it. I'm telling you. Don't wait for it," he advised. Jared blushed. "Ah. I used to be shy with the chicks, Jer. Long time ago. Now I don't give a fuck. Women like that - when you don't give a fuck. French chicks, hmmm," he turned it over thoughtfully, as if going through his inventory of experiences.

"Isabelle's a little different. I gotta go slow." Albert shrugged in response and offered Jared some Cheetos. "Anyway, her family is visiting this month. She's invited me to meet them for brunch this

Sunday at the Grand Hotel something-or-other in Bel Air. Wants to show off her American friend."

"Cool. Daddy's loaded. Has to be a good sign, her inviting you to meet them. What kinda business is her dad in?" Albert was pursuing sales again.

In fact, Jared could think of little else but his impending meeting with Isabelle's family. He loved Isabelle, or thought he did. Was it only three weeks ago? He noticed her while he was reading his comics at one of the less pretentious coffee-houses in his West L.A. neighborhood. She was trying to begin *Wuthering Heights*. But she wasn't really concentrating and Jared, to his own surprise, asked her how she liked the book. Wezzering Ayts. Francaises. Tres cute. Clear brown eyes, translucent white skin, pouty, kissable lips. Conservative dress, tiny waist. Shy and friendly. He wanted to take her home and sit her on his bed, make her blush and giggle, impress her with his stillness, his sweetness. Yes. Never kissed her. No. Held her hand once. Warm, moist, closed around, didn't it? Palms and fingers entwined, a subtle reassuring pressure. Jared slammed on the brakes, the station wagon's ass in front of his nose, tires shrieking in protest.

At home, his apartment greeted him like a drunken roommate. Completely disarrayed, demanding attention and affection for itself, unable to return it. They were both lonely, unable to comfort each other. Unread newspapers and magazines lay astride unpaid bills, half-filled notebooks, twice worn socks, food wrappers and coupons that missed the empty waste basket. The small dining table had been converted into a rummage sale. The bathroom and kitchen surfaces had taken on a filmy, rubbery touch while unspeakable hair-balls accreted in the uncharted corners. Jared wondered if he cared about such things and had to admit that he did. He could hear Albert tell him to get a fuckin' clue. He sat on the couch with its broken spring and sighed at the disorder, utterly helpless to lift a finger to change it.

The week-end arrived. Saturday was a horror. There was nowhere that Jared had to be, so he sat immobile, keeping his standing appointment in front of the television. He settled on old Star-Trek episodes, the original. Through his window he heard the tinny sounds of a football stadium crowd boxed inside his neighbor's T.V. The game was tersely punctuated by urgent male voices, his neighbors, throats hoarse with beer and testosterone, their presence hot on Jared's neck, yelling as the cladded players clashed upon the astro-turf, while Mr Spock's arching left eye-brow spoke silent volumes of reproach for all concerned.

At last it was Sunday morning and he rose early to prepare himself. He pulled into the hotel lot with twenty minutes to spare. In the men's room he glanced at himself in his blue blazer and gray slacks. His brown shoes needed shining so he poured water on a towel and rubbed them. The faucet was a tall spout, zinc colored, shiny, a looping curve like a swan's neck. Jared wanted to taste it, feel its smooth, tangy, cleanness on his tongue. That was an impulse; like ones he had all the time, this one sensual, infantile, touching or licking something like a smooth shiny pipe or the smooth underside of a young woman's thigh. He tucked and straightened, stretched a little, sniffed his fingertips, felt the armpit of his shirt, checked his zipper, his shoelaces. Then he moved on and stood before the door where he was to meet Isabelle's family, strangely more bored than nervous.

The door swung open and a middle aged brunette woman wearing lots of make-up smiled gaily at him. "Eh voila, le beau monsieur arrive. Bon jour, bon jour, entrez-vous, entrez-vous!" Well, well, the handsome young man arrives. Hello, hello, come in, come in. Isabelle's mother ushers Jared in. There were six people in the hotel suite including himself. There was Mother and Father, or Betty et Jean-Pierre; the brother, a slender reed of a teen-ager, named Eric, and the shriveled Grandmother, no name, and no reference to whether Mother or Father had claimed her. And Isabelle. Le monsieur, Jean-Pierre, a florid, effusive man in his late fifties, quickly took charge of affairs, making the necessary introductions. Jared shook hands with everyone, finally embracing his beloved Isabelle who stood limply, blushing at his touch, le kiss, cheek a cheek, mmmuh! mmmuh! He could hear the father chuckle and he imagined a sigh of applause erupt from the room. He tore his gaze from the girl and turned to Jean-Pierre who made a sweeping gesture to the table which was heaped with croissants, pastries, smoked fish, pitchers of fresh and steaming urns of coffee.

They were seated and Jared remained the center of attention for the whole morning. How amiable, how agreeable, how good it was, Jared thought, as Monsieur poured first orange juice then coffee for him, giving him an appreciative wink for good measure. The day was light and so was Jared. He sat in the plushest chair, the entire gene pool of the woman he loved before him, sipping orange juice, buttering a croissant, tasting smoked salmon.

Suddenly, Jared was seized by the impulse to take his glass and fling the contents straight into Monsieur Jean-Pierre's face.

It was a mere thought at first, yet he felt like he had to hold his glass tightly lest he commit the deed.

Throw the orange juice straight into her father's face! Throw it in his face! Do it!

Then what?

"It was such a lovely day, yesterday," the mother began in English with a melodious accent. "Zer was a car-nee-vahl at ze beech. Where was it?"

"Ve-nees", Jean-Pierre said.

"Venice beach. Right. So many people. Zer was music and people doing ze roller ...how you say. All dressed, eh, you know..." she laughed at this point, a disarming laugh.

Jared relaxed the grip on his glass. "That sounds like Venice" he chimed in. He wondered what her face would look like with orange juice dripping all over her make up.

"Oh yes!" and she had a go at describing the weight lifters of all people. "They were really super, so big, you know. Like you, hein, Jean-Pierre." To Jared's astonishment, Jean-Pierre flexed his muscles inside his pin-striped shirt, then chuckled and winked at his family, then at Jared. "And what did you do yesterday, Jer-reed?"

"Ah. Me. Well." he began, folding and unfolding his hands. "Not so much. Took a walk. Did some reading. Had dinner with a friend."

"You didn't spend ze whole day outside? Ah, but you took a walk at least. So beautiful. No clouds, you know. Nussing!" Betty

57

waved her hands as if to brush away the suggestion of clouds. Jared liked clouds.

"Yes, yes. Reading." Jean-Pierre picked up. "I believe you met our Isabelle while she was reading, didn't you now." So Isabelle must have told them that! The object of his affection seemed to stare at something beneath the floor. Jared's fingers gently caressed, teased his glass of orange juice, then quickly downed it. Monsieur, sitting closest to him just as quickly refilled it.

"Wuthering Heights," said Jared, "I remember", he smiled.

"And what are you reading now?" le Monsieur, Isabelles's father asked with interest. Penthouse. Gallery. People Magazine. "...Crime and Punishment," remembering a book he had actually finished in high-school and re-read during his two years in college.

"Ah hah!" rejoined the father, eyes narrowing, "A great book. A great book!" he repeated. "Eric, you read that last year, no? Crime et Chatiment."

"No." Eric replied. Isabelle giggled. Jared looked her way but could not meet her eyes. She was sitting furthest away from him and had not said a word to him all morning. He attempted to look dignified, tingling as he laid his fingers on his glass of O.J.

"Ah..." Jean-Pierre dismissed his son, turning back to Jared, "It is a very interesting study, a very interesting study about...about ze struggle between man's free will to power and his moral conscience," he spoke slowly, allowing time for his English to catch up with his thoughts.

"It is also about...redeeming...redemption," said Isabelle, speaking for the first time.

"Indeed," rejoined Jared loudly, trying to catch her glance.

"Well...I myself never read it," Betty exclaimed, cutting Jean-Pierre as he was puckering his lips to speak again, "So let's talk about something else!" and Madame asked Monsieur to break out the champagne. The talk fizzed on. Jared sat back and occasionally traded witty observations about life in Los Angeles, tourists, etcete-rah. Monsieur Jean-Pierre laughed heavily, winked, as Jared thought to himself, My God, I cannot stop thinking about flinging champagne in his face. His hand felt jumpy, his face a warm blush.

And then the thought became clearer to him. He sat with it. I could really do it. I could actually hurl this champagne into this man's face. Everything is going so well, yet I could fling champagne into his face. It was such an inexplicably outrageous thing to do that the idea utterly compelled him. A flick of the wrist. That's all. And then everything would be different. Fling champagne into Isabelle's father's face! Impossible! Yet so easy. Like stepping off a curb, like jumping off a cliff more like it. A quick, simple irreversible action that changed everything, didn't it? Everything! Jared smiled, a sense of power rising in him. "American people," Jean-Pierre was saying, "they talk about freedom, but not everyone knows what it means to be free, do you know what I mean?"

"You mean," Jared answered, "that all of us behave the way society expects us to. Do what other people expect us to do?

"...Yes. That is correct. I have many American friends who stay in jobs they hate, live where zey do not like. In France it is the same way except that people are not as disappointed. And yet, there are some people, uniquely...American, who go...zer own way. I think."

If he flung the champagne into the man's face, what then? Absolute confusion. Horror. Maybe even denial. Nobody would know what to do. Jared felt like he could punch a hole right through the wall of his own reality. With one simple action he could do it; he could transcend every expectation, break every rule. His hand worked the fizzing glass. This was not crazy Al, happy-go-lucky, propositioning babes, insulting prospects. This was no impulse, no accident. This was opportunity, something creative. This was life on the edge!

"Well now, Jean-Pierre," in broke Madame Betty, "that is all very good, but all freedom has its responsibilities" she enunciated with a French rhythm.

"Responsibilities. Yes, I know of them." He turned back to Jared. "As you see, I have my family, Jer-reed. These are responsibilities, but...good things too, you know. We make choices to have a family... to work hard....to care about what others think of us. Yes? We are responsible for our own actions. Is this a burden? Does it make us less free or more free?"

Wouldn't flinging champagne into this silly man's face prove that Jared was truly free? Free to break from the existence that bound him. His job, his apartment, his timidity, he could walk away from all that. He felt as if he must have known that his life would simply continue the way it always had, the same little rituals, the same little defeats, the same sighing. If he were to do this thing, this very thing - flick his wrist - fling champagne into Jean-Pierre's face, *everything* would change. He would now and forever - here's that word again - *transcend* everything that he had known. He would punch a hole through his existence. He would know no fear. Surely a brand new world was waiting for him.

"Maybe we can do what we want," Madame shot in, "but I also believe zat zer are...laws. Not human laws. Zer are laws...how you say, truz, greater zan us. Ozerwise wisout responsibility we would all go crrazzy in ze street."

Jared blanched, dumbfounded. Jean-Pierre came to the rescue. "My wife is very religious you know," as if she wasn't there. "The fact is, we do not all go crazy in the street and I would agree that most of us do things or don't do things, not because they are afraid that they weel be punished, but because... we accept certain responsibilities." Jared leaned forward, half expecting Jean-Pierre's benediction upon his bubbling heart. "But so often, we feel that we have to do...this thing." he cut his hand across the air. "We don't bother to look...at ourselves. It is a very hard thing to do. We don't look to see who we really are, how we really feel, what we really want. We don't stop to say 'this is my life'. Eh?"

"Absolutely!" Jared ejaculated. This is my life! My life! And he grabs his glass in a cold sweat and flings the fermented drink squarely into Monsieur Jean-Pierre's face! That's it! I did it! I did it! It's done! Free, at last!

The room collapses into stunned silence. Jean-Pierre let out a muffled start, sputtered, and closed his eyes. His entire face was wet, the smell of damp, sour clothing upon him. Jared sat still, his eyes blazing, full of horror and wonder. For seconds or hours, the family wrestled with itself about how to react. It was the little grandmother who finally spoke up, "Baf! Mon Dieu, qu'est-ce tu fais? Qu'est-ce qui se passe!" My God, what are you doing! What's happening!

60

The new life had begun. Everything else had been shed away. All the rules were broken. It was time to make his own. And yet, Jared just sat there, immobile, waiting. Eric finally spoke. "Papa! Mais t'es fou ou quoi, mec!" he said turning to Jared. Man, are you crazy, or what! Jared grinned back at him, round eyed, ready to lunge forward. Or pass out. Isabelle raises some napkins and tends to her father without looking at Jared. Everyone stays relatively calm. Jared remains impassive, heart pounding slowly. Isabelle catches Jared's glance and flees the room. So what! I don't need you! I'm free! Eric and grandmother continued to mutter in French, and another voice rises up, Madame Betty's voice. She speaks quietly to her husband, then turns to Jared with saucer eyes and open mouth, not yet speaking, unsure whether to curse or administer care as if to a sick person. "Jared," she finally begins. "....Are you alright?..."

Jean-Pierre broke the silence, wiping himself off with perfect equanimity, and saying to her in French, "Betty, I can assure you that I am perfectly alright." He sniffed noisily and eased himself further into his chair. He yawned. Jared remained still.

"Get out," she said quietly. "Degage," she repeated in French, her face unchanging, her composure hanging by a thread. "Get out of here. Stay away from my daughter." She enunciated. That was Jared's cue. He was told what to do. It made perfect sense to him, the only sense. He got up and hesitating just for a second he bowed slightly in both the direction of Monsieur et Madame. Eric took his frail grandmother by the hand and led her away protesting softly in a language that sounded neither French nor anything else. Jared bowed once more. "Dehors! Out!" Madame said, this time louder. Jared's heart squeezed with painful pleasure and throbbing erection. He half desired Madame to lose control, to shriek, to rip off her clothes and throw them, then herself upon him. Instead she continued her fixed and crazed stare.

Monsieur Jean-Pierre, without looking up, raised his hand lazily, softly saying, "Salut" Bye. So long. Jared dared to smile just ever so slightly.

"Get out, sale espece de connard!" Get out, you dirty bastard! Jared's rectum blew in triumph, taking over, soiling his backside with a rich and filthy compost.

The conversation had moved on. Jean-Pierre and Eric were speaking in French to each other. The son was making some conclusion, puffing his lips, grinning at his dad. "Ah, yes" the father responded in English. "Well, maybe when you get around to reading Crime and Punishment like the rest of your class did, then you'll have a better idea of what you are talking about." Everyone laughed at this, including Grandma, who laughed not because she understood, but because everyone else laughed. Eric himself shrugged good-naturedly, raising his arms to plead no contest, that the book had no pictures and he was too busy playing basketball anyway to read it.

"You see," Jean-Pierre said, turning to Jared again, winking. "We always have a choice. But sometimes we are stuck with that choice. There may be... no turning back. We cannot always...control or even know our possibilities. But... choose we must. Hopefully we can build upon these choices. Know ourselves a little better. We choose well with breakfast today, no?"

Jared nodded nipped with gratitude. He leans forward to show his attention, knocking his half-empty glass over. "Whoops! Heh, heh." Jean-Pierre chuckled. Isabelle bursts out laughing. Jared glares at her.

"Are you alright?" sang Madame Betty, noticing his pallor, her voice yet merry.

"Oh yes, thank you. I'm terribly sorry." He picked up the glass. There was a small spreading pool of wetness on the empty tray, a little on the hotel carpet.

"Ah, what for Jer-reed." intoned Jean-Pierre, handing Jared a napkin, "We don't cry over a little spilled champagne, ein? Heh-heh."

Jared walked out into the early afternoon sunshine, Monsieur's hearty hand-shake still resonating in his hand. The sky was a perfect dome. His stomach was full and cozy. He might go to the beach, or he might go clean his room, or he might go home and napsturbate, a small veil of Sunday left before the reliable Monday routine of filling customer orders and routing complaints. He thought he might at least be glad to be rid of that silly bitch, Isabelle, prissy thing. He lets the car-doors open out and he turned on the fan to start cooling off the car's inside. He pulls off his jacket and throws it in the back. Maybe pick up some hefty bags at least for the apartment. There were a couple of friends that he hadn't seen or called in quite a long time. Maybe he'd give them a call, suggest a beer or two, and find out how they had been.

COMFORTING ARMS

The Friday Horoscope in the local paper read: GEMINI (May 21 - June 21) 'You are worthy of financial success - and it comes when you know exactly what you want and develop a plan you can stick with.' Indeed, nodded Mary Anne with satisfaction. She sipped her morning coffee, leaving a purple lip-print upon the cup. The horoscope continued, violently shifting its emphasis. 'The quickest way to eliminate bitterness is to forgive.' Her eyes narrowed slightly, the cup hesitating in her fingers. Her head cocked to one side, her pretty helmet of brown hair hanging down. She laid the paper and the coffee gently on her desk. A tidy stack of unopened envelopes piled high for days sat to her right. The telephone with its call display flashed hot white three buttons at a time. The quickest way to eliminate bitterness is to forgive. Mary Anne pursed her lips, drew a breath and held it tightly for a moment. She might have just as easily have written this statement herself as merely read it. As you get older you learn to ignore and get past the little games people like to play with you. You have to let all of that go, as much as that was.

"Mary Anne. I need help with these phones. Line three, O.K.?"

She turned in her chair facing Sidney, the slack jawed clerk, two tables away. "Excuse me, Sidney? Are you talking to me?" she asked in her most even tones.

Sidney punched the third line on his phone, chewed the name of the firm in autonomic greeting followed by 'Please hold', punching more buttons. He looked up wide-eyed at Mary Anne who met his glance straight on.

"Sidney, how long have I been here now?" she asked him as if he had ambled by to discuss it with her,

"I've been here nearly a month", she answered in her sweetest tones, "And you should know by now that when I first arrive in the morning.." but Sidney had looked away and punched in the other line,

64

transferred a call, punched another one in, apologizing to a client, pushing the glasses back upon his face.

The smile fell from Mary Anne. Interesting, she thought of this casual rudeness. Well. When I first arrive in the morning I always drink my morning coffee and read my paper, she muttered almost out loud. I don't need to take any abuse from you, she thought, then considering her horoscope decided to let the slight bounce off of her. And she calmly gathered her paper, her coffee cup, and walked calmly across the office and into the kitchen. Let that show Sidney if he could tell her what to do.

She slowly poured herself a fresh cup, her stomach still burning from the last one. An office of her own might have been a little unrealistic but certainly it would reduce the stress of her job. She felt cramped, boxed in by the jumble of chairs, desks, phone-banks, and computers of the open office. It was so good for her to take her time in the morning, to gather herself to meet the rush of the day, to build upon a quiet moment better to greet chaos with serenity. And if you could do that you could make the world a better place not only for yourself but for others. She sifted through the paper, added two table-spoons of sugar this time and a dollop of cream until her coffee tasted like a See's candy sucker. She turned the paper over, eyes sliding over the economic reports, Senate debates, natural disasters, crack-pot dictators oppressing the masses in far off lands. Then she read about three Mar Vista couples harassed by an anonymous caller accusing them of child abuse to the authorities. She chuckled at the folly of the world, the stupidity of ordinary people.

Her eyes fell upon a story about sickly kittens that had been put to sleep by the local animal pound authorities. She shut the paper with a thud and closed her eyes. Now she was upset and needed an extra minute. At length, she found herself by the coffee pot, filling her cup, sipping it black behind a tingling lightness of being. She washed the newspaper ink, with deeper disgust, from her fingertips. Those poor little kittens she thought to herself, pleased that she had an open heart that could be moved.

The phones were quiet as she walked back to her desk but Mrs. Williams, tall and straight, was standing there, the stack of envelopes that were on Mary Anne's desk tucked underneath her arm with difficulty.

"Hello Betty," Mary Anne flashed her a smile, singing her name. "It's been a busy morning." Betty Williams gave her a sheepish little smile in return. She was so uptight. Looked great, like herself, Mary Anne thought, dressed well, took care of herself, so over composed and coiffed as if the woman thought she could compensate for her natural lack of beauty. It was easy to be nice to her even if she had to take direction from her now and again on behalf of the partners. Mary Anne was a team player.

"Hi Mary Anne. Yes, good morning. Mr. Peterson asked if you could see him this morning?"

"Scott wanted to see me?" she said softly in a high voice. "All right. Well tell him I'll definitely drop in on him before lunch. O.K? It's quite busy, you know." she smiled.

"Yes, I do. But he's in his office right now and I think he needs you right away."

Mary Anne glanced at the files underneath the other woman's arm. "Betty, are you taking those papers? I was going to have some of them filed downtown today."

"Oh yes, well some of them are quite urgent you know, so Mr. Peterson and the other partners asked me to expedite them."

"Oh? That's strange. Well, I was going to do that anyway, but if you really want to do my job for me," and she smiled opening her mouth, raising her brows and her hands.

Betty Williams laughed, waving her hands. "Sometimes it just works out that way. Anyway, Mr. Peterson is expecting you right away. He wants to see you before his ten o'clock meeting." And she left, Mary Anne looking at her back, Sidney bending his head down further into his work.

Well then. The boss wants to see me right away. Even on such a busy day. She smiles to herself, pleased that her worth has not gone unnoticed. She pops her head in the door, knocking as she opens it, vaguely hoping to catch him at something. "Scott? You wanted to see me?"

"Ah, Miss Thomas. Larry, let me call you back in an hour. Uh-huh, O.K." and Mr. Peterson hung up the phone glancing at his watch. "Yes. Come on in. Please, sit down." he offered, swiveling front in his chair.

"I can come back later Scott if that's better for you. I know you're quite busy and I've got plenty to do myself."

"No, no. Now is perfect. Please have a seat. Actually, why don't you close the door first while you're still up," but she had already sat down so he got up himself and closed the door without further ceremony. "I'll get right to the point," he began sitting down again. Mary Anne gave him her sweetest, most attentive look, aware that her blue eyes must have beamed at him irresistibly. Peterson hesitated. He held up a pen and beat it slowly as he started to speak. "It's difficult for me to say this, but I don't think that we're a match for each other, you and our organization," he let out a sigh and leaned forward taking off his spectacles. "It is our observation that you are not happy here with your work. So in the best interests of not just us but yourself as well, I think we should both move on and let you go. I'm sorry."

She looked at him squarely first nodding slowly then shaking her head. "Of course," Mr. Peterson continued looking off, "You won't have any problem collecting unemployment plus we'll give you a week's severance which is not bad considering you've only been with us a short while. Also, if you'll allow me to say, with your resume and interviewing skills, I'm absolutely sure that you'll have no problem finding another situation that better suits your needs and talents," he concluded, hoping that she would detect no irony in his voice.

"I see, Mr. Peterson" Mary Anne began. "I guess...I really can see why this would be difficult for you."

"It's never easy."

"I guess not. Come on Scott," she said mildly, "You're afraid that we're not a match for each other? Isn't that interesting the way you put that?"

"Miss Thomas?"

"This isn't about my work here for you, is it Scott," she spoke icily, tiny eyes, letting out words like chunks of metallic ice. "Why can't you be honest with me? I know what really goes on between the two of us. And you're the one who feels uncomfortable and out of place."

"What?"

"You're threatened, that's what it is."

"You have the work-habits of a spoiled teen-ager!" the partner bursts out. "You barely finish anything and you are disruptive to others."

"I'm not interested in you Scott, you got that?" she shouted. "When are you going to face reality? Reality, Scott. Ever hear of it?"

"I have a meeting to go to Miss Thomas" Peterson announced, rising to his feet, pressing a button beneath the intercom. "This discussion is concluded. Since you are obviously upset I'll have Greg and Stanley assist you in packing your things. Ms. Williams will bring you your check."

"Oh really, Scott."

"Mr. Peterson."

"You're calling security now? I'll bet that makes you feel really powerful," she said evenly, eyes like slits.

"It saves time," he says curtly, a light film of controlled sweat beading on his forehead. "As I said, I'm sure that you will find something better suited to your needs in no time," he added, this time openly sympathizing with the woman's past and future employers.

"Oh, I will, I will," she said. "And I sure have learned a lot from working with you lawyers. Speaking of which you'll be sure to hear from mine tomorrow morning. *Scott*!" and she turned on her heel and walked past the security guards at the door.

She was proud of the way she had handled herself. No one was going to walk over her ever again. Was it justice for her to be fired because she refused to sleep with the boss, a married man, even though she might have wanted to if she had been allowed to move up at the firm, and if she had become absolutely convinced that he really wasn't so happily married after all. And all that was beside the point. The main thing was this; she had stood up for herself. And even better, she had refused to lose her temper or even get angry. She might even try to forgive Scotty, maybe not right away, but soon to avoid being bitter, like her horoscope, the stars, advised her. She would forgive, but she would still pursue the lawsuit, out of principle, in defense of other women, as well as herself. Maybe she would even get one of the other partners in the firm to take her case, she thought, eyes twinkling. Wouldn't that be a rich burn?

The day improved as she was able to make a last minute lunch date with her best friend, Joanie, who she had not seen in several months. "Look at you. You only call me when something like this happens. My god, Mary Anne. Good for you for standing up to him like that. What are you gonna do?" says Joanie, nails wagging, her black dyed hair tied in a scarf.

Mary Anne sighed. "You know Joanie. Maybe it is the best thing. But I've been so depressed lately. It really just doesn't seem fair. And it's like I've had this funny feeling, I just *knew* this was coming."

"I'll bet."

"But you know there is one good thing," she smiled. "My horoscope affirmed that I am worthy of financial success. And you know, I am. It was so nice to see that in my little fate this morning. Don't you think?" and she winked and patted Joanie's hand, raising her cocktail to her lips, glancing at her friend, measuring the response.

"Uh-huh."

"I really think that fate's trying to tell me that I didn't really need this job. That something better is out there for me."

"Well hon, that's a great attitude."

"Isn't it? Besides, as a lawyer, there are all kinds of opportunities out there for me. An attorney can go anywhere."

"An attorney?"

"Mm-hmm. Sure. Well. You know, I've worked in enough law offices over the years. I'm sure I know more than most of these fat slobs behind their big desks."

Joanie knitted her brows, "Now you're actually a legal secretary, right?"

"Lawyer, legal secretary, the law, it's all the same. *I* say I'm a lawyer."

"Well honey, I admire your confidence. I wish I had it. But my husband's a lawyer, not that I'm always proud of it. You do know they are not the same thing. Be proud to be a legal secretary, hon, it'll be a lot easier for you," she said with a wink of her hand. Mary Anne smiled silently at her. "Come to think of it, maybe I can ask him for you what kind of a harassment case you got."

"Why thank you Joanie," she said so gently. "Thank you for making that distinction for me between a lawyer and a legal secretary. What would I do without you?" she continued smacking her drink down on her half empty plate. "I wonder why you thought it necessary to bring it to my attention. Perhaps it gives you satisfaction to talk down to or should I say 'advise' other people. Takes away from looking at yourself doesn't it," she rose, her chair scraping behind her. "Speaking of which, you really should do something with your hair. You have a mirror at home, don't you *hon*?" She asked with concern. The other woman made a confused protest but Mary Anne continued, from a great moral height, "Maybe we can talk again when you can learn how to be supporting instead of attacking." Then she announced that she had another appointment and quickly left before the check came.

Who needed Joanie? Two, three times a year they see each other and immediately the woman thinks that she can tell Mary Anne how to run her life. Now I'll do something for myself. So she saw a matinee, telling the cashier that her boyfriend would meet her there looking up and down the aisle for him to arrive in case anyone was watching. After, she wandered innocently unnoticed into another feature down the hall. Walking out, she felt as if days might have passed, as if she had awakened surprised from a long sleep. What a day. Through adversity you begin to see things more clearly. You begin to see people's real motives, who your friends are. She began to see better than ever before the little lies that people tell themselves, the power games, the judgement, and above all the hidden anger and resentment of people. This day was yet another trial for her and once again, she was proving herself strong and resilient, able to take care of herself, able to face her problems head-on, she thought as reeled into the parking lot.

She ran little errands, did some shopping, got things done. The sky hung low, closed in like a lowered ceiling. Mary Anne defiantly tried to keep her shoulders from bowing beneath it. Returning to the house later than usual she found Petra, the teen-age girl who looked after things after school dozing in front of the T.V. set, her notebook on her lap, legs sprawled on the ottoman. She quickly roused herself as Mary Anne shut the door. "Any trouble? Did the kitties eat O.K.? Here sweetie, kitty-kitty-kitty?" she rang. Everybody has eaten, yes ma'am. Everything was quiet, no trouble, Tweety, Boxer, and Allison were all checked on, no problem. "Goooooooooood," she said cooing at the cats. "Melissa" she continued confusing her with the previous girl she fired for stealing, "Please take your shoes off if you're going to put them on the ottoman, alright?" she asked in a friendly way.

"Yes, ma'am. I'm sorry." And Mary Anne dismissed Petra, sweetly docking her only an hour for sleeping. Afterward, she counted the change jar to make sure the girl hadn't been in it. She quickly changed into her bathrobe settled in front of the television and ate a bag of micro-wave popcorn, no butter, and a plain scotch, no soda, kitties crawling all over her. She would think of what to do tomorrow she decided. She'd get up on Monday, go to the unemployment office, ask about legal action. A loud thump came from upstairs. Mary Anne looked up. The ceiling creaked slightly from someone running across the floor. Ah, she sighed. Her day was never ending. Just once during the week she'd like to come home and have no further responsibilities. She decided to go up and see what was happening. The door to the second bedroom was slightly ajar.

She opened the door to find a little girl of about six in her P.J.s sitting on the floor with a worn-out looking stuffed dog in front of her. The little girl had just hit the dog on the nose and was pointing her finger at it when she looked up moon-eyed at her mother.

Mary Anne sighed with folded arms. "Isn't it a little bit past your bed-time?" The girl scampered into bed clutching the little dog to her, tucking herself deep inside the covers in a placating way. Mary Anne walked over to the bed, looming huge and stiff, shadows crisscrossing her face. She leaned over, heavy faced, drew a breath and kissed the little girl lightly on the forehead. "Now Allison," she said quietly, "Don't you think we're just a little bit old to be sleeping with stuffed animals?" Allison shook her head, then stopped, shrugged.

"Give me the dog."

"Nooooh," the word squealed out of the girl like air screaming from a tire. "Pleeeeze," and her face collapsed in on itself, the mouth contorting outward, the dog ripped from her grasp.

"I've had a long day, Allison! The last thing I need is your goddamn whining. You're a big girl now and your gonna have to start growing up, you got that. You want me to throw this thing away?" The girl was already wet with tears. "Allison," the woman continued this time very quietly, smiling with infinite patience, waving the dog gently by the neck in her left hand. "You don't want mommy to get mad now, do you? You know I can't stand it when you cry."

The girl sniffed, shrugged, and shook her head again looking back at her mother with deep set eyes. "O.K. very good. It's time that you starting growing up now. I'm taking the dog away now to help you grow up. O.K? You understand? You do understand, right?" The girl looked down and nodded. "Look at me Allison," she said raising her voice by a soap shaving. "That's all right then. You do understand?" The girl look up wide-eyed and nodded.

71

And Mary Anne left, putting the dog in the dusty upper closet. To throw it away, she thinks, would have been cruel. She poured another drink and was about to fall asleep when she knew she had to use the bathroom. Forgetting about the guest bathroom she plodded heavily upstairs, and almost knocked the toilet seat off while trying to sit down. Regaining herself, she threw water upon herself and was about to turn to her own bedroom when she heard a sound, a muttering coming from the girl's room. Quietly, Mary Anne crept down the darkened hall, nearly losing her balance before finding the wall. Allison's door, still slightly ajar, opened silently against Mary Anne's touch. From the ghostly light of the T.V. downstairs, the little girl could be seen on her knees bent forward over the bed, head down, hands together in front pointing upward.

"What are you doing out of bed!" Mary Anne shouted. The girl let out a scream and scrambled under the covers, supplicant. "Were you praying!" Mary Anne pursued, "I said, are you praying! Of course you were. You were praying, God Dammit!" ignoring the little girl's silent denials. " Praying for what? Allison? Praying for what? And to Whom?" she slurred. "Praying for God to deliver you from your evil, rotten mother? Isn't that it you hateful little bitch!" And she kicked the bed, rousing a heavy throating sobs from beneath the bed. "You're praying for God to come and get me, aren't you? Aren't you! You little shit. You're trying to set God against me. Well guess what. Guess what," she sneered, make-up running down her puffy face. "There is no God! You got that? There's no God. There's just you and me here you little idiot and I've got to do everything for myself," she screamed slapping the shivering lump in the bed. The girl barely felt the blows, like being slapped with floppy pillows. Yet her mother's curses rang between her ears like a great shovel emptying the heavens of all the furry stuffed animals, of all the comforting arms from above. Yet she prayed on in spite of herself, praying to a tiny point of light weaving away from behind her clenched eyes. "There's no God." Mary Anne spat out her words, already exhausted, "Another one of your father's lies." and she kicked the bed again. "You'd better stop praying Allison. Cause I'll know if you do. You hear me," she raised up again and ripped the blanket from the girl in disgust, throwing it to the floor and storming out without noticing that her daughter was still balled up, her hands still together.

Mary Anne plodded downstairs again and flopped in front of the T.V. again where Petra had dozed. She called out for Tweety and Boxer, but they were nowhere in sight. The muffled cries of the little girl played on. Mary Anne crouched in the comfort chair, the world shrinking to six inches above the hand with the drink in it. The rest of her day crept in.

She thinks of all the ungrateful, phony little people at work where, she was glad to have quit them on her own terms. Her phony baloney friend, jealous, flaunting her lawyer husband, maybe even afraid Mary Anne might steal him, she thought belching. Even the way the ticket people looked at her; odd, knowingly, snot-faces. The newspapers and their terrible tales were perfect justice perhaps for such a world. She thought of the distant dictators. Who knew what pressures had caused him to take the steps he did, to forge order out of chaos? The strong man promised to take care of everyone in the land. Hearing her own daughter still whimpering she cut the urge to shout from below, though she sank down at the thought. She stiffened against the pain. Her drink was empty. The world shrank to a dark, hardened point. How she resented all the toys and the God above that intruded to take care of her little daughter. Where, or where, she gasped in the darkness, were the comforting arms to take care of her?

PUSHED

1.

Even after Johnson was pushed out in front of the on-coming subway, he still had a surprising amount of time to take stock of his situation. Freed from the necessity of having to take protective action, his consciousness was allowed to free float, sometimes fixing upon multiple subjects, sometimes upon nothing at all, though struggle and resist he continued. Johnson wondered if it had all been a dream and would he now wake-up in his own warm bed staring heavy lidded and tousel headed at his own clock radio. How many countless times had he woken up before, just as he was falling, falling, this time surely for real, to his doom, when in the next instant he felt himself hugging his pillow, inert, safe, all forgiven for the moment. Such hopes were badly used at Johnson's odd recollection of unmistakable details of his last few moments prior to his predicament; the smell of chestnuts, funky and black as they grill cooked on the street, a greasy puddle near the subway entrance way, the canary piss yellow dirty color of the rusty turnstile whose metal arms he routinely jumped that day and every day. Then there was the big, huge, black hair of the big Latina lady in the purple dress whose rumba he was picturing in his samba, oh so nice. She was big and crude and rude for sure with lots of make-up, a big burlesque package deal, and goddamned if he hadn't been looking for her again not paying attention to anything else when his body jerked into the air head long into the train, as if God Himself had flung him out. For not paying attention. Of course. You should have been paying attention! Now look at you. Was anyone else being flung out? Perhaps. Or maybe he had intended to jump anyway.

Instantaneously Johnson felt an overpowering sense of shame. This shame was so great it crowded out even his terror. The thought that possessed him was not so much, 'I am going to die a horrible, painful death and experience nothing more after', as much as, 'How stupid, how stupid, how stupid.' Then another voice instantly told him, I must have deserved this. Moreover, it was not true that Johnson's life passed before his eyes, except for the sad, reproachful glance from his mother who became ill when he was still just five years old.

More desperate to impose order rather than grace upon his final moments, Johnson summoned the instant image of a terrible stem growing from his mother's sighing disappointments to his own imminent demise. The notion that his trajectory with the oncoming train was fate, a curse from everything defeating about his life, skipping over what was happy, rather than a ridiculous accident somehow actually lessened his terror and sense of loss. He felt once more closer to his God, even if He was a damning rather than a saving sort of deity. And that is how Johnson's shame overwhelmed his terror. Though in almost the same exact moment something else happened, something that changed everything and something he could not have anticipated.

Just before the moment of impact, if only for the tiniest graceful instant, Johnson felt the most profound boredom. As if, how could I be bothered with all this train business! Once when Johnson had to play a lengthy violin solo for his high school recital, almost moments earlier he had suffered the most brutal fear of disgracing himself before his peers and parents. In the next minute, just before his solo, he could barely keep his eyes open so great was his sudden disinterest and drowsiness. He went on to play flawlessly. Now that blissful sleep, that sweet boredom, this was mercy at its cleanest, he stopped wriggling, and arms open as if in an embrace flew into the thunderous shaft like a boy diving into a wave. He barely heard the shouts of the onlookers mixing with the rush of the train, a single thrusting noise, one of encouragement, cheering him on to his challenge, except that he and the train were united in the same cause, were united like lovers and would see this thing through to the other side. He was doing his part. Now the train would do its own part.

The moment of impact was flawless. A clean gargantuan obliteration! It was everything. The universe was no more. Just before that instant, as bored as he was, Johnson knew that the impact couldn't hurt and it didn't, except for a cold, blank feeling, and the strange idea that he now had a second head. This wasn't so bad, he thought in zero time, perhaps I'll come through with a slight concussion. If only he could keep still. If only the train wouldn't keep hitting him.

He was hit first across then down then over his body, moved and bent at impossible angles, his back and neck flying over his head while his chin, depressing his chest and legs flying against joints in the other direction. All was blank and muffled except for the notion of being folded over and over into smaller and smaller rolls, first the size of a suitcase, then a bread basket, then a can of tuna. Yes, Johnson was at last nothing more than a can of tuna, compressed tightly, tightly. And he was still and felt nothing. But a slight echo. He realized without knowing "he" or "Johnson" or even the train, that he did not feel so compressed. For that was the only thing that he could remember, was that he was compressed though he thought not in any such words. Yet there remained the impression that once he was compressed and now he was open, though without any size that one could detect.

For a flicker a human emotion remained. A touch without sensation felt its way in, the womb without size before it had a human attached, and a baby's sob might have emerged from him, relief, of course, of course, of course. But then everything was out of bounds from all such thoughts and words, and lazy like a leaf it fell resting gently upon the soil, a seed undifferentiated from its moorings.

THE WAY TO NOD

They say it is just over three hundred miles from Soho to Nod, yet the distance for most people might as well be the same as from the planet to its sun. Nor could any two cities possibly be more different. Both are major settlements in the vast southern desert land of Sudo, an oft forgotten protectorate of the Classical Empire. Both are reported to be inhabited mainly by a slender, beautiful people, as dark as the gaps between the stars in the heavens and with eyes as blue as the endless skies vaulting forever into nothingness.

Both cities harbor networks of underground caves and catacombs where substantial sectors of the population reside. Both cities are sustained by deep underground wells of rushing water, whose source is mysterious, yet thought to come from distant mountains of mammoth proportions. These similarities, however, are vastly outweighed by overwhelming differences.

The most obvious difference is size. Nod supports a relatively modest (and often invisible) population of perhaps a quarter of a million souls (or so they say), whereas Soho is a monstrous behemoth nearly twenty times that size. The silent, chalk white adobes of Nod sit immovable, impervious to the distant maelstrom throbbing through the charcoal labyrinths and blackened ironworks of Soho. The streets of Nod are always empty at midday and the silence is nearly total much of the time. The heavens above are also radically different. The murky, brown mists lapping the dark and twisted towers of Soho exist in violent contradistinction to the endless, impenetrable blue sky that lords over Nod. Nod is a land of light, even underground, whereas Soho is shrouded in shadow, even upon its highest rooftops.

Though many speak in admiration of Nod's quiet beauty, its Mosaics and tiled frescoes, its fountains, its sanctuaries and gardens, it can also be a disquieting place for first time visitors, few though they may be. The rare traveler from the Empire reports feeling anxiety amidst the exceptional quiet. The broad and unpaved boulevards, flanked by

77

immaculate cloud white buildings, stretch in silence for miles. Seemingly abandoned yet immaculate city squares feature perfectly maintained fountains built upon dazzling turquoise, marble and stone, cascading the purest well water, the steady lone sound in the unchanging afternoons. Colonnades arch over pristine terra cotta walkways. Everywhere is the sky, the deep almost cobalt blue solid sky. Signs of life and activity can be found in courtyards and curving stairwells and hidden market places and cafes. The only times when people congregate on the boulevards are at sunrise, sunset, and at midnight. Then supposedly the people come in large numbers, some in the white robes of the novitiate, others in silk caftans of many colors depicting arcane symbols, and still others strutted in the soldiers garb, loose fitting crimson slacks, leather boots, brilliant sabers glistening in their belts, though no wars or battles have been fought in that region in recorded memory. The men drink tea and argue and laugh ferociously all night long, though nary a fight every broke out amongst them.

Nod is a place of great scholars and poet philosophers. A few become religious teachers, others life-long mendicants, possessing quiet healing powers. Others became holy fools and magicians who live and die of their own choosing in the eternal desert, having gone mad as forgotten troglodytes. But mostly Nod is a land of order, where chaos is discreet and contained in the steamy, jasmine tea rooms where bearded men discussed astronomy, poetry, and mathematics. Immaculate markets sell unaccountable quantities of fresh spices, nuts, olives, and salted fish and dried meats of every variety. Nod is a city of libraries and archives great and small, of quiet scriveners and of chapels and meditation rooms on every corner and behind every courtyard, and of monasteries of every variety encircling and embracing the city.

Soho by contrast is a tangle of great serpentine towers, teeming at its surface with thousands of appalling markets, nameless narrow alleys and illicit businesses of every size. Women were not to be envied. Those that were not bought and sold in the markets walked covered in black robes, faceless and shapeless, like specters. Men and boys lowered their eyes at them. They stared instead without shame at the young, bony girls in the smoky dens and lounges, lost females with their cavernous, burning eyes, dancing languid behind glass cages, dangerous and thwarted like sedated panthers.

In the heart of this blackened city it was forever neither day nor night, for by day the sun is shrouded at all times by a massive whirlwind of thick and angry rust colored dust. By night, however, the city is lit up in neon at its center in a rage of commerce and bombast. At its edges, the city is lit up by millions of candles from it millions of lonely, faceless people. Up above, the night sky is pale with its surfeit of halogen projected across the pinioned lake of perennial dust menacing from above.

Without warning, the copper sky itself will descend like a desiccated flood and crash into the city in a great storm of dust that sends all but the most stalwart and foolish for cover into the many miles of public indoor walkways and halls, but even here relief from dust is never secure. Many are caught outside and can merely throw themselves upon the ground to wait it out, breathing through their scarves, and often trampled by others still desperate to escape.

The only relief from this pestilence of crowds and filth is the desert monsoon, a weird and unlikely season of torrential rains that falls for weeks or even months at a time every year in spring and summer and which somehow attaches itself as do the dust storms, directly over Soho. The very few that envisioned escape from the terrible city came to learn that their only hope was during the monsoon. Traverse alone across the empty desert was considered impossible.

From where does the monsoon come? Almost no one at all knows about the existence of the ocean or even what such a marvelous thing actually is. The great southern ocean, warm and violent, roiling salty and seething, somehow pale and electric, embraced the unknown shore not more than fifty miles to the south. The ocean seemed eternal from its first sighting and extends to the ends of the earth.

Most of the people had heard of the mountains far to the north, terrifying yet revered, which are reputed to be the source of Soho's fresh water underground lakes and rivers. The ocean rains themselves were acid and sour. It was instead the mountains that gave life. They were like Gods, severe, remote, yet powerful. More than a few humble souls who lived on the outskirts succumbed to losing themselves, gazing forever upon them.

When the cold mountain winds met the warm ocean vapors, the monsoon appeared. Like magic they formed rivers of mud that flowed and often flooded the merciless alleyways. Finally the mud was washed away and the ironworks seemed to shine and the air was fit to breathe again. The wealthy retreated to their lairs up above in the towers, while the vast numbers of the poor came out and walked the streets and prayed and let themselves be drenched by the warm, sour rain.

∞

The old man did not look well. But neither did she. No man would have her and she felt grateful for this. At first glance she looked to be a withered old woman though she was barely nineteen. If you cared to look more closely you could easily see past the lines in her face and bear witness to her feral beauty which she herself did everything to hide. Her father was indeed quite old. He was forty-two. They say that the rich looked greased up, soft and fat and lived even into their fifties and sixties, but the common folk could do little to escape the excesses of dust and heat. The old man, her father, had worked as a porter in the bazaars for many years in the inner city while his daughter, Fatima had managed to live with another family in the outskirts. He lived behind a curtain in a tiny clay room in one of the many blocks of catacomb like apartments that lined the inner city. Here he claimed he had all the privacy he needed. The room was furnished only with weaved blankets, a pillow, and a glowing bulb that hung from the ceiling and turned itself off at midnight. Once a week, Fatima came to see him and he would give her what money he could. They sit upon the blankets against the soft walls. But this week, she asks for nothing and instead she hands him back a thick wad of bills.

He looked at her in alarm. "What is the meaning of this?"
"Do not worry about it father. It is for your health."
"You need this money. You must have it."
"I have enough. Everyone pitched in."
"Do they know?"
"Only those I trust the most."
"Oh. But those are the ones you must be the most careful with."
"I have to trust some people."
"I suppose."
"Most of it is actually yours. Your money"
"What are you talking about?"

"You gave it to me. And I kept it. But I am more worried about you then you should be about me."

He trembled. "But don't you need my money?"

"I have you, Papa. I have you."

"Not for long, though."

"Do not say that. You are with me always. And everywhere."

"Ah. Yes. And you are with me."

"I love you, Papa."

"Are you alright?"

"Yes, Papa."

"You promise?"

"I'm leaving tonight. Now. That's what I came to tell you."

"Tonight?"

"Yes. You knew I was leaving soon."

"I...I did." She holds his hands in hers and then she kisses them and she smiles and all the lines and creases of her young face are summoned at once. She is a sad, old woman, yet very beautiful. And father and daughter take each other's hands and they lean into one another, their foreheads together, and there they sit, their eyes closed, asking that this moment may be present with them always. The old man wanted more than anything to hold her forever, to tell her not to go, to tell her how much he would miss her, how empty his life would be without her. But he did not. He did not want to burden or suppress her. He knew how she felt. Long ago he had tried to dissuade her but all it did was make her angry and more determined. He came to admire her. He understood perfectly. There was no future here. Not for anyone. Least of all for women like her. But what awaited her beyond? Could it be any worse? What if it was? A lot worse? She had explained and he could not dispute that she had to try. Fatima had already learned all there was to possibly learn in this place and the rest of her days would surely be in decline and less and less likely on her own terms. Best case scenario she would marry a wealthy man and live at the top of the towers. More likely she would marry poor and end up in the iron works or dying young from consumption or God forbid she might end up as a slave underground held hostage because of her husband's debts or even for no reason at all. How selfish would he be to try and deny her escape from such a futile life, even more so since he would be dead soon enough himself. So he began to give her money, what little he had and it was the

81

best that he could do. But now she was giving it all back to him. He vowed never to spend it. But he would keep it to remember her by. It was all that he had left of her.

There were times when he had been ashamed to bring her into this world at all. He himself had not had it nearly so bad as many others did. He had escaped the ironworks. For years he had served tea to the rich but then came the time that he had had to haul heavy loads all day long and his back was bent. At last he was allowed to stop working and to enter into what they called your wandering retirement.

He held his daughter for a long time. He believed in God. He could not help it. The rich did not believe in God. But they were happy that poor people should believe. The old man believed but he did not know what he believed in. If God loved us all then he must be very weak indeed to let us live like this. Or perhaps instead he let us all suffer because otherwise we would never follow him. The last thing he said to his daughter in a croaking voice was simply this.

"Fatima, you are the most beautiful being in this universe. Be safe." No other words would come. She embraced and kissed him and then hurried from behind the curtain disappearing quickly into the midst of the banal voices, the coughing and lazy laughter, and the clattering dishes from the myriad of families in his midst. He waited until he could be sure that he would not see her if he succumbed to opening the curtain.

The old man wept all night, exactly as he expected he would. The rain kept him company and he dreamed all night of his daughter and how beautiful she was and he prayed constantly and he felt unworthy and finally he slept for a short time just before the early dawn. It was raining still. He rose and changed out his tunic. He put the money from his daughter in his shoes and he walked upon it and thought of her and made his way to the communal fountain just barely underground. There he washed himself as best he could and he prayed and he wept and people were kind and asked him about his sorrow and he declined to speak for he did not know if he should speak of his troubles. It was as if he believed there were spies who might denounce him or capture his daughter. But the truth was that he was surrounded by weak and wizened old men exactly like himself.

Weeks went by. Mostly, he was alone, but at noon every day, the old men in simple airy gray caves below each tower all met and trudged slowly in a circle, usually around a chalky gray fountain, dry and dull, sitting mutely in the center. Slats of light shafted through. They prayed but they did not know to what they were praying or even if whatever it was they prayed to could hear them or act at all. Mostly they were silent and together. After they trudged in silence about the fountain, they faced each other in a circle and they held hands and they chanted at their own pace, chanted for mercy, chanted for peace, chanted that their sadness might be heard and that there might still be beauty in this world. Silence then descended like a curtain upon them until they were brought back to life by the gathering monsoon. How they loved the rain, for it negated the city and chased away the dust.

The markets had all moved indoors. One day he walked with his companions Rafi and Tariq, men he had often walked and eaten with, yet about whom he still knew very little. Neither of them ever spoke very much. Both of them were even smaller and more emaciated to behold then he was. Tariq walked with a stick. He was still in his twenties yet he looked as old as the old man himself, or maybe older. The three men stooped inside a tunnel and emerged onto a level of perfectly non-descript residences where Tariq sometimes lived amongst several families. It was time for the noon day meal. Not everyone was there. Some had been called to the ironworks and would only be home on the weekends, blackened by the smelted dust, coughing themselves to sleep all day and all night. Tariq had once worked in the ironworks and often he himself still woke up coughing.

Everyone in the apartment – women, children, and old men - sat upon blankets and talked or grunted and no one minded being jostled up against each other for they were all like very young brothers and sisters together, yet comforting and parenting each other and there were fifteen or sixteen people in all, the old man estimated. The many children smiled and crowded together and wrestled each other amiably and none of them had any idea how small and weak they really were. Some were already asleep in each other's laps. Everyone, adults and children alike, was given the chance to wash his hands and to give blessings. Each was handed a bowl with a salty gruel and something like fried dough to wipe up the remains, which was warm and satisfying but often still had flecks of grit and sand within it. And the old man had his bowl refilled for him and the toothy matron, a sweet and awkward beauty of maybe sixteen or seventeen nodded and smiled at him and indicated that it did her honor for him to eat not just one but two bowls from her humble fire. There was gentle laughter all around at nothing at all and for a time they forgot their troubles for during the monsoon there was often little to do but they were lucky that they had their store of food and sometimes random strangers would come about as well and these too were fed. And everyone was wizened and ugly and had rivulets of dust chiseled into the creases of their shriveled faces and no one knew or cared about that one bit for these were not their troubles at all. For if you were here it meant that you were not trapped below in the ironworks or even worse in the flesh pits that had devoured so many of their daughters and even their sons. Life was still simple as long as there were people who had enough food to share.

   After the meal was over, some people left but many more stayed and lay down and slept nestled against each other and it was all just in time for the crescendo of the afternoon monsoon and the old man's heart was lighter for a moment and he wished he was once again with Fatima and the thought made him sad and proud. When he awoke with a start, he examined his feet, but his shoes were still on and the money was still there and he lay back down again for a short time, but then it was Tariq who put his bony hand on the old man's shoulder and while the others all slept, he and Tariq quietly made their way down to the communal cesspools. Every man hung his tunic and made his way naked to one of hundreds of holes over which he squatted and eliminated as nature commanded. On rare occasions someone would slip and fall but only a very few holes were large enough for a man to disappear through. It had been known to happen and if so, there was nothing to be done. One had to be careful. That is the last way I intend to go, he thinks, but nevertheless how fitting. It was not too difficult to stay alive, though. Rumor had it that more than a few had actually chosen to end their lives this way. The old man shuddered. He and Tariq retrieved their tunics. Often enough one ended up with someone else's tunic or even had to go about naked until he could reach his own shelter. No one paid any attention if they spotted a scrawny old man walking about the caves or terraces naked. It was only a problem if such a person had no other clothing at home.

   "Let us go to the baths," Tariq suggested afterwards.

"No. I don't feel much like it."

"Well, do you mind if I take a quick one myself?"

"That's fine."

Tariq gave him a sidelong glance but said nothing. They descended a level and made their way in the dark, grasping at the clay walls, the warm sulfurous smell of the underground springs assaulting them. Tariq's limp seems suddenly more pronounced and he leans ever more, quivering upon his cane. They both can hear the murmur of hundreds, maybe thousands of older men. "It's strong today, the sulfur. You sure you won't partake?"

"No. I'd prefer not." The old man is unimpressed with the smell of sulfur mixed with the pungent smell of unwashed and withered flesh.

"You'd prefer not. I see. No matter. You won't mind if I have a quick bath."

"Do as you please."

"You'll wait for me."

"Of course. Where else do I need to be?" And so the old man sat on the narrow stone ledge in the shadowy cave in the midst of a mammoth lair of sulfur steaming springs which seem to glow and pulse with a feathery amber light. "Be careful. They might be too hot."

"I'm always careful," Tariq mutters and he gingerly makes his way to the first pool where several old men wade at the edge of the spring. Many pools are indeed too hot to bathe in, but many of the men like it very hot. Tariq feels the water with his hand and he looks up and gives the old man a look. "You're right. This is too hot. But I know where the waters are a little cooler, and where it isn't so crowded."

"The baths are always crowded, Tariq." The old man smiles at him.

"I know a place," Tariq insists. And he grips his stick and taps it, his back bent over, his hand trembling to hold it in place. He walks back over to the old man. "Ah. Let's go," he says impatiently. "I know the way. There are some smaller caverns more poorly lit so they are quieter. A man can think or relax without being surrounded."

"Fine. But let's go slowly."

"We'll be careful. It's not far."

They cross over shallow streams along the way. Tariq takes off his shoes. "You know it is less slippery if you take your shoes off. Some of these floors here are made of clay."

85

"I'm fine," the old man replies while stepping gingerly across the narrow gaps.

"And more pleasant for your feet, you must know."

"Too much trouble. I'll be fine," he says, regretting now his decision to come in the first place.

"Suit yourself."

Slowly they pass through chamber upon chamber, a baffling and dangerous maze for any initiate to ever navigate, yet they trudge along, seeming indifferent to the labyrinth. "Down here."

"OK." They descend down a very narrow passage and into a dimly lit cavern with a shallow flow of warm water and a little shelf conveniently jutting from the wall. The two men sit and listen to the waters. No one else is within sight and the sounds of other men are muted and far away. "Impressive. I presume you've been here before."

"Yes, of course."

The old man looks at his friend though he can barely make out the man's features. "Tell me then. Is everything well with you? You seem troubled."

Tariq fails to answer right away. "You ask me if everything is well. You know very well that all is not well. Not in a place like this."

"Then why did you bring me here?"

"Please! I mean our entire world. At least as we know it."

"Yes, of course. I should have known."

"This is all we know, but can this be all there is?"

The old man sighs. "Must we talk of this again?"

"But what else is there really to talk about? What else is there that could possibly matter?"

"I'm an old man, Tariq. I try not to trouble myself."

"At least answer me. Isn't there more to this world?"

"I hope so," he says, thinking of his daughter.

"But will we ever know of it?"

"I don't know. You and I, we probably won't."

"If I had the chance, I would leave."

"I know. But you've already survived the worst that this place can put upon us. You'll never have to go back to the ironworks, my friend. They leave us alone now, for the most part. We all rather look after each other. We come and go as we please."

86

"Well it pleases me to leave this place altogether. Maybe if you had had to toil below for years, you would not be so content."

"But where would you go?"

"Where then has your daughter gone to?"

"Oh...." The old man hesitated. "I did not want to speak of that."

"So it's true. She has left us?"

"I just told you, I did not want to speak of that."

"But why not? How can you ignore such a thing?"

"I ignore nothing, Tariq!" And he coughs into his arm until he can steady himself. He sniffs, eyes watering, looking down. "It is all I ever think about."

"My friend," says Tariq, putting a gentle hand on the old man's shoulder. "If she is already gone, how can it hurt to share what you know with me? I am happy for your daughter. But now I want to do the same."

"Ach!" the old man sits up straight. "How do you know such a thing anyway?"

"Do you really think that such a thing can escape notice?"

"Yes. I was hoping very much that this would be the case. My daughter's business is her business."

"Such a thing is of great importance to all of us. Obviously she told enough people so that some of us know. We must all have hope of following her to freedom."

"I can only pray that freedom is what awaits her."

"You don't think so."

"Fatima did what she had to do. As I said, I can only pray for her."

"Perhaps you are a man of little imagination."

"This is all I know. For Fatima's sake, I hope there is more."

"You're an ignorant old man, my friend. Of course there is a whole world out there. Have you not even been to the outskirts? You can actually see the sky! It is a bright bold and brilliant thing, empty and pure, colored like nothing I have ever seen before. And at night there are such marvelous glories in the sky that you would fall to your knees."

"Yes, I know. It is beautiful. Beautiful and utterly unattainable. Everyone knows that."

"Why dismiss that? Surely it must mean that there is more to this world than dust storms and ironworks and the gluttonous appetites of the Elect!"

"Do not say that name allowed!"

"What are you so afraid of, old man?"

"I have looked out at the land beyond the last buildings. You say I am ignorant, but I have seen for myself. Nothing! There's nothing at all out there. There can be no greater nothing than such nothing as faces you there!"

"And what of the mountains? Have you never seen the mountains? What of the empire we have always heard of. I tell you that there are hundreds of cities and places out there where the land itself is brighter and more colorful than our most wonderful blankets and carpets. I have even heard from some of a marvelous vast body of water, endless to behold, that leads to many, many wonderful new lands, if only one can build some kind of vessel to carry it forward."

"Now who is ignorant? What a fantastic story! Even if such a body of water existed, it could only mean the death of anyone foolish enough to place himself upon it."

Tariq was silent for a moment. The old man could no longer make out his features yet dimly he hears his voice. "If you really believe all that, then you must truly be grieving for your daughter for you are a man without hope."

The old man sighs. "What is it that you want from me, friend?"

Tariq leans in towards the old man. "I have been making my own inquiries for quite some time. I am almost certain about my next course of action. But I want to be completely certain."

"You and I both live in a place of complete certainty. Every day is like the last, except for the coming and going of the monsoon. No?"

"What is this place that your daughter seeks?"

He closes his eyes. "It is a city that is supposed to be not too far away. Far, but not too far. I don't know."

"But what is the name? It must have a name."

"Would you go there?"

"I might. May I not inhabit the same city as your daughter?"

The old man smiles, but the smile fades quickly and Tariq can barely see it. "Nod. It is a place called Nod."

"Nod?"

"If it exists at all."

"How could you let your daughter leave if you do not even believe in such a place?"

"How could I stop her? I could not…But nor would I do so even if I could. She is a woman now. I have done all I can do."

Tariq nods. He grimly reflects that it is far too late for him to ever have or raise a daughter. "Tell me about this place."

He spoke as though far away, his voice rough and broken. "She said it is a quiet place, a clean place. There are….white walls, fountains. The sky is clean. I can't remember what else she said."

"Time is short."

"Time is long, Tariq. Too long."

"That is because you have no hope." The old man does not respond. He sits motionless in this dark corner with the rush of the shallow aquifer rolling past. Tariq speaks again, "I am considering your case, Zaqir Taz."

"What is there to consider?"

"Will you not go there yourself? To be with your daughter? I could understand that."

"I am too old to…." The old man does not finish his sentence. Shouts and echoes abstractly pass and ring through the hollow chambers.

"Maybe you are older than I am. But look at me. You see me?"

"I see nothing. This is a place of shadows, my friend."

"You have seen me! You have looked upon me. This is what seven years in the ironworks does to a man. You have been lucky. You are blessed, Zaqir Taz!"

The old man can see just the outlines of his companion, frail, hand trembling on his cane. "Yes. Yes. That's true. I suppose I forget. But now that is done! You are free of all that now. Why do you agitate yourself like this?"

"Ah, isn't it easy for you to tell me that I am free. You truly know nothing about me, after all."

The old man shakes his head. "Perhaps it is time for us to go."

"Why is it that you never take off your shoes?"

"My shoes?"

"You wade through the water in your leathers. At nap today, you kept them on. All day. And this is not the first time. Every day that we meet it is like this. But I have said nothing."

"Then why say something now?"

"It is not natural. Do your feet afflict you?"

"My feet are of no concern to you."

"So you will not answer my question?"

The old man rouses himself to sit up straight. "Let us go, Tariq. I do not wish to have this conversation with you."

"Why should you take offense? Am I not simply asking about your health, Zaqir Taz?"

"Only you alone can know what it is in your head and in your heart at this moment." The old man struggles to stand up. "Shall we go? I will need your help to navigate back to where we came in."

"How much money do you have in your shoe?"

The old man looks at Tariq and wearily sits back down again. "Do you really mean to rob me my old friend?"

"Would you suspect me of robbing you if you really thought of me as your friend?"

"You are my friend as are all of us who are simple and poor, as are all of us who share this space and walk these halls. We are all friends." His voice sounds small and unconvincing.

"There are many things you do not understand, Zaqir Taz. Your life has been easy compared to mine. You will never know."

"And what if it is? Are we to compete regarding our suffering? Am I now one of the..." he lowers his voice. "Am I now one of the Elect in your view?"

"You need not lower your voice in here. There are no censors down here."

"I am suffering right now. You know very well!"

"And what if you are? You still have no wish to leave this place. You say you pine for your daughter, yet you won't lift a finger to be with her. Even though you have the very means to leave. And I would praise you for going to your daughter now!"

"I do not need your praise!"

"And I say you do not need that money that fills your shoe!"

"Ah..." the old man looks down. Almost in a whisper he says, "So you do intend to rob me."

"Those of us who still dream of something better, who dream of freedom; we who dream like that, well we know that such freedom is not for free."

"It is if you steal it!" The old man laughs but he feels exhausted already by this horrible exchange. "Take me at once away from this place Tariq and I shall burden you no more with my inferior dreams."

90

"You need not mock me. And you do not need that money for your food and you know it. I am at my wits' end, Zaqir Taz. Though I am younger than you, I still have less time left to me in this life. Perhaps it is not too late for me to know some peace."

"You will never know peace, Tariq Bal," the old man mutters. "Not like this. And the only place better than this for you is the grave."

"What did you say?"

"You heard me, Tariq. Now please, either rob me now or take me back to the surface. I am simply worn out by your disgraceful pronouncements." It is all that the old man can do to forcefully and levelly make his statement. For a moment the only thing that either man can do is to listen to each other's labored breathing. Finally, the old man looks up with his weak, rheumy eyes and hazards a smile and changes his tone. "Come now, then. Haven't we been through enough already? We are all worn out. At least we can both enjoy what little we can before the monsoon either ends or floods us out. We are not yet so broken. We still stand where many others have fallen. Let us then go up and enjoy the rain. I have a sack of some of that dried, smoky food you like. Maybe we'll even have a smoke. Yes? Ah, let's do that. And perhaps you can even rob me later." And he chuckles to himself and coughs. The old man cannot even see Tariq, save for the silhouette of a trembling hand that seeks to hold steady his walking stick. The waters continue to flow more deeply now as the run off from the rain is allowed to funnel down. Both men breathe more deeply. At last, Tariq speaks.

"I am mortified, Zaqir Taz that you would call me a thief."

"Oh....I am sorry. I am not-"

"Please do not justify yourself."

"I am sorry, I am sorry. It was just my frustration with the strange way you were speaking. Let us both be calm and speak logically."

"Please do not patronize me. You have called me a thief. That is plain enough."

"Enough!" the old man finally explodes and attempts to rise, but Tariq brings his walking stick down on his head though with such feeble force that Zaqir Taz begins to laugh again. Again, Tariq attempts to swat the old man with his staff as much as his withered bony arms can muster. The old man laughs and puts out his hands. "Please Tariq. Before you hurt yourself or act much more the fool, let us come together like men

91

and go to the district where I will buy you dinner and something to smoke. Yes?"

In response, Tariq continues, almost mechanically it seems, to bring his stick down upon the old man, mostly missing him and causing the old man to laugh further which only infuriates Tariq even more. Zaqir Taz opens his mouth to speak and raises his hand when Tariq finally brings his stick down with sufficient crack and accuracy to suddenly silence the old man. Before the assailant can take this in, he is already continuing to bludgeon his victim, several sharp blows in succession, quickly making his pledge darkly irreversible. Finally, he stops.

There is only the shallow sulfurous stream. Tariq cannot even see the old man, though he knows exactly where he is. He waits. He breathes heavily. He calls out the other's name. Then again. And again. Just to be sure. Then he watches himself explain to the earthly remains of Zaqir Taz what he is about to do.

Tariq speaks in low measured tones, thanking Zaqir Taz yet mildly admonishing him as well, lecturing him and speaking of acceptance of all things, and promising finally to find the old man's daughter so as to bestow a father's everlasting blessing. All of it is of course utter nonsense, he realizes but it helps to keep him moving forward and to understand the brand new world he now inhabits. He kneels before the body and to any random passerby in that great subterranean cistern labyrinth, to anyone catching a glimpse in the dim stony light, it might have appeared that Tariq was washing the feet of another, perhaps a holy man, praying and whispering praises. In fact Tariq was carefully removing the old man's shoes, first the one, then the other, and in one of them indeed the money was all there, just as he had imagined. He felt a tepid relief as he spotted it and he picked it up, a mass of flat and semi-congealed greasy bills bearing the arcane symbols of the state in reds and golds.

At last it was time to leave. But how was he to carry this money? He deliberated for a time, for he wore sandals instead of the regular shoes sometimes worn by people with means. Neither he nor the old man however had any pockets. All things had to be carried. He cursed himself for not thinking this through until he had arrived at a workable though distasteful solution. Tariq removed the tunic from Zaqir Taz, muttering respectful prayers, and apologizing for having to leave him naked in this place. He then placed the money carefully inside the folds of the old man's tunic and carried it as a bundle under one arm, while in the other he leaned once more on his walking stick and from there climbed the short embankment to where many men wandered in the very dim, steamy light in search of the next pool or stream.

∞

He decided he had to act at once and indeed there were no more ties for him to this world, no obligations, no more friends, and never any family. He sets out to leave at once, grasping to remember all that he has been told. Of course it had to be the same place where he and the old man's daughter were going. At last he had the means to do so and he vowed that he would leave in honor of Zaqir Taz and seek out the man's daughter to praise her on the old man's behalf.

Suddenly he was very tired yet he willed himself to go on. He emerged upon the main level where the monsoon was in full reign. It came down and even blew towards him from where he hid against a great iron pillar. When the rains were at their greatest, the markets retreated inward. He followed several passage-ways, some crowded, some not, all great stony tunnels that narrowed and opened until he reached the outer edges of the market place itself. This was a place of many lights, all of them disembodied, mere projections, however bright, advertisements for all manner of wares and entertainments, most of which were free to him as a veteran of the iron works, though little good this did him since they most often never existed.

On occasion, holographs would suddenly appear featuring many writhing dancers and singers as well as strange and random patterns and information. The censers free floated, simple and fuzzy orbs of red light that passed on through everyone. Tariq knew that such surveillance often resulted in arrests and disappearances, though he could not be sure what triggered these. He doubted it was for the detection of ordinary violent crime. Certainly it was not to keep its citizenry from indulging in spontaneous expressions of obscene passion with each other. He worried that such a considerable amount of cash spirited in the old man's tunic might trigger an alert. Suddenly, Tariq turned from the virtual tumult as well as the actual crush of beings and turning to his right, all quickly became darkness. The reach of the censers was oddly limited to commercial areas.

Here in this dark yet familiar pavilion sat and lay the many thousands during the communal siesta that took place at all hours of the day or night. Many kinds of lucid dreaming took place for hours each day, induced by communal pipe smoking and by the large luminous images above that seemed to float in the artificial blackness up above, images of beautiful, voluptuous and well-oiled dancing girls. A low moaning or hum haunted him, emanating from everywhere, the undisturbed breathing of the feeble unwakened.

Tariq passes along as fast as he can, hobbling upon his stick, clinging to his bundle. Here he was little worried that anyone would rob him for everyone here was already robbed of earthly ambition. Tariq's feet began to trouble him. He knew he was headed for the corridors. Several skinny men stand in the first few corridors, naked but for a sheet wrapped upon their withered organs, hunched with narrow pot bellies, standing against the chalky walls, grinning at him, stupid and vacant, barely a jagged tooth in their heads, greenish skin in the phantom light. The smell intensifies as the passage way narrows. Here lie many dozens of mutant, deformed, or diseased sentient beings, some missing arms and legs, some with faces bloated or obscure, or with open wounds, some perhaps long dead. There were few if any doors but limitless hallways it seemed, each one more slanting downward, more receding and narrow than the last.

There were times when he walked in near total darkness, surrounded by the sounds and shuffles of the random multitudes. He emerges onto a very large plaza, sometimes illuminated and sometimes in darkness. From the smell, then from the agony of the downpour he could tell he was outside once more, beneath some dilapidated colonnade, still plunged in darkness, the rain impassable, the streets finally empty, and Tariq would scurry as best he could like an injured rodent through the dank and abandoned arcades. He turns a corner and listens to the storm and he feels the lash of hot rain upon his face and he recedes against the wall and is struck by an unaccustomed moment of wonder at the sourceless monsoon exploding from the imminent sky.

Onward he hobbles, picking his way, tapping his stick, finding a stairwell that leads upward. He curses the darkness but no candle would serve him even if he had one. There is nothing to do but to use his stick to make out the steps and their curves and slowly he climbs, touching the roughhewn walls. He counts to ten over and over, expecting not to measure, but to lose himself in the act. It is not so far and he finds a torch light that leads him to a lonely walkway. Here it is that he looks for yet another stairway, only this one will lead him down again and very far indeed. But before he can reach it, he anticipates that he will have to pass within sight of the upper iron works. Slowly he moves feeling stiff and soaked in his joints, clinging to the dead man's bundle. Well my friend, Zaqir Taz. It appears we are still together. With a little luck, we will both be on our way to find your daughter. Somehow this new thought of bringing Zaqir Taz with him in spirit to find his daughter brings comfort to Tariq, as though he were pleased with his generosity of spirit and was moreover even long suffering in lugging along with him the dead man's garment as well as all his earthly wealth. Dimly, Tariq retains the knowledge that this conceit is false, yet he adopts it whole as necessary to keep him focused on his task. There will be time enough later for soul searching. For the moment there is only Tariq and Zaqir Taz and the monsoon. And soon he will find the right stairwell down to where his rare passage outward can be purchased. Suddenly to his right, across the darkened plaza, an unlikely giant plume of flame rises, carrying with it a miserable groaning of metal grinding like a great falling beast, accompanied by anonymous shouts either of glee or of panic. Mutely he curses all that he sees. Tongues of fire dance up the twisted towers setting the ironworks aglow. In the light of the flame, Tariq recognizes three miserable apertures up ahead, like crouching punctures in the clay. He shuffles up to them and peers inside of each. Two of them lead only to lost blackness while the third reveals a dim set of stone steps, steeply spiraling downward. Tariq sits down, eyes watering, assessing his task, estimating he can lean against the cavern walls as he descends. He clings to his bundle and to his stick and he very slowly descends, mindful that every step could be his last. Once more he begins to count, mindless and empty.

Nothing exists but the step before him, the air pungent with unknown water borne life, the walls glistening with seeping, vivid moisture, his rickety stepping down still lit by the iron fires up above. One more step. And then another. And then comes the darkness as he descends too far for the light from above to penetrate down here. Even

95

the monsoon is already gone. The only sound is the distant echo of dripping from somewhere below. Much closer is his own labored breath. There is no handrail. He sits in the dark. Well, my Zaqir Taz, what shall we do now? This is the chance we take for hope. And a moment later. Do not chide me. This is the way. I have always walked these ways and I have heard many times what others have told me, even if you never did. But still. We go. I take only you with me. I have hope. And you have your daughter. Let us go find her then.

From his seated position, slowly he finds his footing and step by step, clinging to his bundle, probing with his stick, he descends one more step and one more step further beyond the point of no return. Counting. Counting. He had forgotten long ago how to pray and to what he should pray. So all that is left is to count in the dark. I have seen the iron works for the last time, he thinks to himself. Faster he edges himself downward until the glow from the ironworks is replaced by a deeper red glow from the steamy, pungent level he now passes through, a transient subterranean plane with no sign of people. Deeper he passes. He wonders, what if I am too late? What if I have gone too far? What if I am in the right place, but they send me away, or they are not even there? How foolish I am not to make better inquiries. Perhaps such a venture could drag on for a very long time. But no. It had to be done and it had to be done now. There was no other way. He was utterly committed. How could he forget? There was absolutely no place for him to go. All he had was nothing at all, a communal rug to sleep upon, forever in a different spot, at best inside a dimly lit clay hovel above ground, warm and full of sickly children with ragged teeth, watery, cavernous eyes and sad smiles. Afternoons after the meal - if lucky, some warm gruel with cabbage and onions and weak chilies - he would lay upon the carpets, sometimes with Zaqir Taz, and the children would often nap right up beside him warming his bones. They would call him Uncle and say they were sorry whenever he shushed them for giggling or wrestling and he would feel bad for being impatient with them, for so ruthlessly mitigating against their modest joy. He could always sleep, for this was the one great luxury still afforded the people, which was to lie down, never in privacy, in communal apartments, in tiny alcoves behind beaded curtains or ragged rags, or amongst great multitudes of strangers who sleep in the great market place seeking out lucid escapes. In dreams we were never strangers except for that singular moment of awakening which all beings

96

had to do on their own. Beds as such were unknown except amongst the Elect but sleep was granted and even encouraged to all who were no longer indentured to the ironworks or to the flesh markets in payment of petty, infinite debts.

He opens his eyes. He's back on the underground stairwell. Stay focused. He must find his way out. He must find Fatima. Yes, my Zaqir Taz, there is no turning back. Let us find her together. Slowly once more he makes his way further down one step, one step, one more step at a time. No one will stop him. But if I should fall and mangle myself no one will help me. This is where he would remain, the world forever lost to him. Tariq continues to inch his way down to the next step, slowly descending, hearing the waters at last and the faint hive of human activity. Am I dreaming? It fades in and out. There it is again. One more step and another.

He rests and dozes and more than once he awakens having believed he was moving further but he had only dreamed it. Imagine that, he thinks, even in my dreams I am still right here! I could be anywhere, even in Nod. But no, I am still here. Or am I in fact dreaming right now! He doesn't want to waste precious effort by descending in his sleep, nor does he want to sleep at all as tired as he is, so Tariq decides to test himself by slapping his thigh. Nothing. I must be dreaming. Or am I just numb? Or did I miss it? He slaps himself again. It sufficiently stings to satisfy him. But what of it? What of that son of a bastard, Tio Amir, the one who told him the way? Did the man despise him after all and lead him to die down here?

After what might be minutes or hours, he hears the unmistakable sound of people in commerce and leisure, shouting and working. He wonders yet again, Am I dreaming? He successfully counts from one to ten, and then he does so a second time; Tariq knows that he never has and that he never could have counted in his sleep, so therefore he must be awake. One more step and another and by the next step a soft glow falls upon the step below. At last he picks up his pace as the light grows stronger. Tariq tucks his bundle and gathers his stick to slowly raise himself up, trembling and leaning against the wall. Keep going.

Before him is a walkway that stretches limitlessly to his left and to his right as well as to about ten or fifteen paces in front of him. Beyond these dozen or so paces, there appears to him a great trench carved in a gully, stretching the length of ten human bodies, Tariq

97

estimates. Upon the other side is yet another walkway exactly like the one before him. Everywhere up high there is colored halogen and neon lights bold against the darkness.

All is brightly lit with endless rows of tiny shops and vending stalls. The people look about the same down here as up above, perhaps slightly better fed, their skin smoother and paler, their clothing newer, wearing exotic pantaloons and chemises. From where had they all come? Surely they did not all come from that same dismal aperture from which he had just now descended. There must be hundreds or thousands of such apertures and more than likely great majestic staircases or mysterious conveyances throughout the city.

Tio Amir had been very clear and very precise as to how Tariq should find his man. Every week he would find Tio in the same corner of the Dream Confectionary and they would chat while the others lay steeped in dreams. "Yes, Tariq, this is how it is done. When will you be ready?"

And Tariq would always reply, "When I have the money."

"And when will that be?"

"God willing, in this lifetime."

Tio would laugh and say, "That is very pious of you, friend. But you should protect your investment my friend," referring to the small amount that Tariq had already paid him up front.

"You are certain of all this?"

"Ah, Tariq, how many times must I assure you? And how many times have you asked? And it is always the same answer. But I understand. No one trusts anyone anymore."

"When did they ever?"

"You and I go back a long way." The two men had labored together in the ironworks, but only briefly. Somehow or another, Tio Amir had escaped this servitude after barely a few months, a circumstance that Tariq often wondered about. After his own release seven years later, Tariq was too weak to work anymore, but his friend had become a dream concierge, bearing witness to the long afternoon of sleepers on their communal mats; withered old men and frustrated young ones who dreamed their lives away. Tariq had had enough of all that.

"Why don't you go yourself, Tio? Why are you still even here? You don't even try to fool yourself with this nonsense here that you keep watch over."

98

"I'm not going."

"But why?"

"I have a companion, have you forgotten? And she will not go."

"Ah yes, your companion. How tender. She does not mind your long absences in the flesh markets?"

"Please, Tariq. You speak outside the bounds of what should be spoken. We must have some decorum." Companions were rare. Tariq wondered if he ever really wanted one. His only companion was his goal of escaping to the bright, blue sky to the clean fountains and white adobe buildings and the quiet, orderly avenues.

"Tio Amir. Now who is acting pious? But yes, congratulations on your companion, for you were strong and young enough when your servitude was over to engage in such a thing."

"Would you begrudge me the meager happiness that I have?"

"I begrudge no one anything. Please," said Tariq hotly with forced and oily confidence. "I think it is the markets themselves that keep you here. That is what you do with my so called investment as you say."

Tio grins and says in his smoothest voice, "Shall I repeat once more how to find your man? Will that finally satisfy you?"

"Yes. Yes," Tariq answers, softening his tone. "Even though I do not yet have the means. That is always what I want to hear."

"I tell you what, my friend. For free – anytime - I will take you to your final destination my self. To your ultimate freedom. Even right now." And he puts out his arm and points with his hand to where the dreamers are dreaming.

Tariq looks at the great hall of dreamers. He trembles and his heart feels heavy. He waves his hand dismissively. "No. Not like that. Not even you believe in that. I would go there with my eyes wide open."

"Suit yourself."

"Just tell me once more. Tell me about how I find my man."

"I will tell you. Yes. Be sure to remember and to be ready to visit him when the next monsoon arrives."

He remembers now that he had doubted Zaqir Taz. Ach! Not Zaqir Taz. He meant Tio Amir. That was the one he had doubted. Not for a moment had he doubted the word of Zaqir Taz, who had been a friend and at times almost like a father to him. Yes. Now that was a man. He was a man of integrity, a man worth defending and following. Tio Amir, on the other hand, was a slippery one even if he did willingly share his company. But so far everything that Tio Amir had told him had come to pass. Or was he still dreaming?

Not so long ago everything was clear and vivid. But once he entered the aperture, he had become more weary and unsure of himself. Yet he knew to turn right now and to walk for about a mile, maybe two. That was what he had been told. Tariq staggers stiffly still clinging to his bundle and to his stick. He marvels at the distant vaulted ceiling and the great, sculpted trench that separates the two lanes. Glancing more closely he sees a brisk rushing of water that flows down the gully, some kind of canal. The walkway is teeming with tiny shops, small grills and tea counters, and little apartments. The shops are all filled with modest rugs and pillows, pipes of all shapes, sizes, and colors, and tobacco of several varieties, small bags of flour, bulbs of onions and other curious roots, vestments and sandals, small and rough pieces of colored jewelry, tiny clay flutes and obscure instruments, as well as random curiosities such as the kind that foment darkly in sealed jars. Tariq was not accustomed to such seeming abundance. He was hungry but he felt frightened about revealing his money, or rather the money entrusted to him by his friend and sponsor, the severe yet venerable Zaqir Taz. Tariq was on a mission to find his man and to find his way out to a better place. As he plods along, marveling at the unreachable markets across the steamy canal, he feels unreal and weightless and the sensation frightens him as if he were about to re-awaken in that dim and lonely stairwell. Everything, however, resembles what Tio Amir had described. Any moment now therefore, the crowds may thin out and the lights will dim a bit and the people will be smaller like him, and poorer and slower as well. All of this comes to pass and soon there are only dark passage ways dimly lit behind thin and grimy curtains.
He passes several cages where razor thin naked young women beckon to him, youthful in their supple movements, though their eyes are sunken and creased, teeth crooked, gums dark, hands scaly like talons. Tariq had heard about these displays from Tio Amir and of course there were many such up above. He considered himself long past such desire yet he indulged in staring at one such writhing, heavy lidded girl. Despite the devastation wracking her face and body she was nevertheless

a great and mesmerizing beauty. He wanted nothing more than to watch her – privately, in a beautiful tiled steam bath such as one could only find amongst the dreaded elect. The girl gazed at him and curled a wretched claw of hers to summon him, the while gazing right through him to a plane far beyond. He broke his eye contact and his heart felt heavy.

Before him now he saw a pale green light that seemed to flicker behind an oily paper curtain. This was what he had been instructed to look for. He began coughing and he suddenly remembered coughing often while still lingering in the stairwell, as if he had been there for a very long time. He became aware of his burdens; his stick and his garment bundle, and his arms had grown stiff and weary. Yet his possessions were his friends and he relied on them, though he was very tired. But very soon everything would change. We are here, my friend. The immaculate and peaceful land of Nod awaits us. Your pure and lovely daughter awaits us. Soon we shall be transported and our troubles as we know them will come to an end. Finally he steps towards the paper curtain. He stands for a long moment in silence in front of it. Echoes of the life down here rattle remotely about his head, casting their calls of commerce, their random shouts, and everything that is the dim soup of distant humanity that forever froths about and beside him yet touches him directly almost never, the effervescent and skimming noise that protects and contains the ever truthful silence that always is beneath and beyond such echoes, the silence that is best obeyed in the midst of the promiscuous din, the eternal nothingness that is itself at last the crown of home, the indestructible place that persists in the midst of impossible dislocation in a land that knows not its home, that knows not itself.

He stands before the curtain. And he hears the waters that rapidly flow through the channel. Hello, he says, as if to himself. I am here. He says it again, this time in utter silence. Hello. I am here. At last he says it out loud at the top of his voice. Ekart Mansour, he shouts. And he pulls aside the curtain and slowly he enters. In the gently throbbing green light he makes out several sleepers. He is used to these. So many people are sleepers, both down here and up above. That is their function, it seems. He passes on to a low ceilinged room, silky green fabrics fare a loose fitting ceiling. Tariq stoops, wanting suddenly to go to sleep himself. A small huddle of men, sit faceless in the minimal light in the corner. Bravely he sits beside them feigning to be part of their

101

group. No one pays attention to him. He speaks. "Please, I am truly sorry to bother any of you. Can you tell me though where I might find Ekart Mansour?

A man finally replies. "Who sent you here?"

"No one."

"Who sent you?"

"Well I was given your name by Zaqir Taz"

"Who?"

"Zaqir Taz."

"The name means nothing to me."

"He was a very great man."

"There are no great men."

"He was a good man."

"I don't know any Zaqir Taz."

"Well you see, he actually set me up through a man named….Tio. Tio Amir."

There was a low chuckle. "Yes, I think I know that fool."

"Can you help me go to…this place called Nod." He pronounces the name with difficulty, as if there were something obscene about the name.

He hears Mansour sigh in the dark. "You're quite serious about what you are doing?"

"I am as serious as it is possible to be."

"Are you?"

"Of course."

"A donation is required."

"Of course." And he searches the folds of his rank and tight little bundle of Zaqir Taz's cloak. He finds the folded greasy packet of long and damp bills and in the greenish darkness he peels off several random notes and blindly offers them forward.

The man takes the bills and holds them up. Satisfied, he pronounces, "It can be done. We can take you away from here to where you want to go. But you cannot come back, at least not the same way. You understand?"

"What is that to me? I have nothing to keep me here. I am nothing here."

Again there is silence between them. Ekart Mansour finally speaks, "What you are in one place, so you shall be in another."

102

"Will you take me to Nod?"

"Leave and come back on the third night. That is when the water once again runs high enough. Come directly here. And I'll take you to where the way begins."

"May I stay here? I have no place to go. Perhaps in the front room?"

"Very well. You can sleep there. That is what it's for." Mansour's companions sit utterly mute like stones. Suddenly Tariq realizes that the silent men really are in fact clay statues. He is in fact alone with Mansour. "Is that all that you have there?"

"Is that not enough?"

"If you mean the money, there may indeed be another donation required. But I was referring specifically to the garment you carry. Do you not have any other possessions?"

"Only my staff. I am a poor man. I slaved in the ironworks. I have nothing."

"I see. You are a man of the mines. Such a man is welcome to lie down in my sleeping room. And indeed you will have little need for more where you are going."

"Thank you. Even the money I have to pay you comes from my friend and sponsor, Zaqir Taz."

Silence. "That is twice that you mention this name to me."

"It is truly because of him that I am here. He wished me to seek out a new life for myself and to carry a message from him to his daughter. He was a good man."

"A good man you say."

"Yes indeed."

"It is too bad that he could not come himself, yes?"

"Yes...yes it is too bad. He was already very old. Over forty years. And ill. It was not for him to leave from this place in this life time."

"Perhaps he will do so in the next one then."

"Yes, perhaps in the next."

"Do you believe in such a thing?"

"Do I believe in what?"

"Do you believe that there is such thing as another life?"

"We have always heard about it."

"Do you believe?"

103

"I don't know."

"Hopefully there is. For the sake of your friend. Right?"

"Yes, for the sake of my friend."

"Then again….perhaps if your friend had decided to come, then who knows, but you yourself then might not have been able to sit here right now in his place. Don't you think?"

"I don't know."

"No?"

"Maybe."

"Yes. Maybe. And what is the name of this man's daughter, the one you say had already left."

"I think it was….I can't remember. But I know it," and Tariq peers into the darkness of his own memory. Then he looks up and with great excitement he pronounces her name. "Fatima. Her name is Fatima." Tariq smiles in the dark. He imagines Mansour doing the same, but he cannot see the man's face.

"Fatima," comes the voice. "And you believe you are honoring this man and his daughter with your presence here today."

"I can only hope."

"You can only hope." They sit in silence for a long time. "Go and sleep then if you like, until it is your turn to leave. There is a bowl of meal and a tureen of water in there. There is a level below you will see for your ablutions. I will summon you when it is time to go."

"Yes. Thank you. Thank you." They sit in silence a moment longer.

"Is there anything else then?"

"Who are these that sit with you? If it is permitted to ask."

"They are my companions of course. They guard this place. They enhance all that happens here. You shall not know their names. Now go."

Tariq bows while seated and he slowly gathers his things and makes his way back into the outer room where he finds an unoccupied matt. Then he finds the stone tureen and ladle for the water. It is surprisingly good and he takes a second full ladle, then a small scoop of the meal which is bland and clay like with small bits of stone but no more than usual. He finds and uses the spittoon and continues eating. All in all, it is a peaceful sort of place. All is quiet except for the breathing of the dreamers, and all despite the walkway so close by. He tucks the garment beneath his head with the rest of his treasure and he lies down feeling very old and tired. Instantly he falls into a very deep sleep. For a long time the only thing that follows him into his dreams is the soft green glow in the dark and a gentle mumbling voice that in his dreams seems soothing instead of afflicting. On occasion he opens his eyes and listens to the snoring of his invisible companions. He closes his eyes again. Eventually he rises and begins a restless journey through small and non-descript chambers, most of them filled with sick and deformed people, sometimes filled with human filth discarded ineffectively, piled in some corner, or stewing in the cracked tureens of brackish water. Suddenly he finds himself alone in a familiar clay stairwell, leaning against the perspiring stony wall, whining pitifully to himself, gazing at his shaking purple hands, croaking the name. Fatima. He touches the cold wall, feels his hand shaking, listens to his own voice call out for her as if her presence was imminent, but he knows that all he really seeks is the bloody cloak with his money. I'm sorry, the high pitched shredded voice ekes out. I'm sorry. And in the very next instant he hears again his companion dreamers, their snores, their breathing. He smiles and he disappears again into sleep, descending stairwell after stairwell, losing himself, now and again staring intently at that purple, shriveled hand in the dark, startling himself awake again in dread.

He is awakened again by his own coughing. There is no day or night down here. He rises, his stomach in knots. He looks about uncertainly. A man whispers to him, startling him and asking if he wishes to use the latrine. Tariq acknowledges that he does and the man leads him to an aperture in the corner lit from below by candles. A ladder made it seems from some kind of toughened hemp leads to a narrow chamber just a few steps below. To his surprise the attendant assists him to find his footing, a tiny hunchback who attempts to smile at him with his loose, fleshy lips. Tariq trembles, a feeble old man now, and he follows the hunchback a few steps to a larger chamber reeking of human waste and filled as well with a silicate powder of limestone. The hunchback instructs him carefully where and how to squat over the drop point, though he is difficult to understand.

Though he suspects he soils himself a bit, Tariq manages to relieve himself. After he is done the hunchback suggests that Tariq help himself to a handful of lime powder with which to wash himself. Tariq begins to weep uncontrollably. He cannot account for this but he accepts the suggestion to wash himself with the powder. The hunchback steps ahead and ambles with amazing agility up the ladder. From the top he coaches in gibberish for Tariq to pull himself up, finally reaching for Tariq's arm with a surprisingly fierce grip. With the hunchback's assistance, Tariq makes it back to the sleeper room and crawls upon the smooth stone floor back to his matting.

Many times and many ways over the countless stretches and undifferentiated green glow of sleepers, Tariq sets out for the land of Nod, longing for the moment when he will arrive at Fatima's door, embracing her in her father's embrace. Together they will pray at last in the clean, eternal sunlight, the pure and haloed ice blue sky laced with shifting wisps of spectral clouds high above the pristine white pavilions set in their polished stones. Tariq and Fatima will smile and they will listen to the singing pristine fountains, the prism rainbow of water cascading and glinting off the shimmering tile. And they shall marvel together at the beauty and at the peace all around them and within and between them. Each moment will last for all time. Each moment will last for all time. And she shall be my bride for I am now a son to my beloved Zaqir Taz. The purple hand quivers before the dark merciless wall and Taqir starts not knowing whether to wake himself up or to cling to his sleep but he struggles like one about to be smothered and he is already sitting when he hears Mansour's voice in his ear.

It is time.

Tariq nods in the dark and he is even helped to his feet. Thank you, he tries to say. Thank you. He trembles all over and he suddenly feels naked. Where is my bundle? Where is my bundle? But he has said nothing after all. Nothing will come out but a distant wheeze. He begins to cough.

"Will you be able to do this, Tio?" For Tio is an endearment shown to strangers of a certain age.

"My bundle?" He hoarsely states. "My bundle?"

"Do not concern yourself."

"Where is it?"

"Do not concern yourself about any lost money. All of that is settled as far as I am concerned. But you have to go now."

"But...my bundle."

"It's alright."

"I can't leave without it."

106

"Perhaps you will not need money where you are going. It seems to do us precious little good here as well."

"But...I will be all alone. I need that tunic. My eternal friend, Zaqir Taz!"

"Listen to me you old fool. You have a place on the vessel. It is here. Yes? But you have to go right now, before I change my mind."

"My brother, my father, Zaqir Taz. How can I?..."

"You can stay here if you prefer and never go to Nod, but dream of it instead. Is that what you want? And never find your precious Fatima, never hold her in the flesh. Or you can come with me right now. I will not ask you again."

"Fatima. Yes. Fatima," and he works his mouth which trembles like a leaf as does the rest of him and he feels chilly and as one who has always been shriveled and naked. Indeed, part of him wishes to remain in the sleeper room forever to dream of the purest white and blue, of the empty, gilded avenue. The purple hand cringes and clenches. He starts into life. "I will go now with you. Yes, yes, of course. Of course. Thank you. Thank you."

"Come then."

And they lead Tariq out of the dim greenish chamber, through a thin little curtain and down a narrow walkway lit by candles. They turn and he feels a cool and not unpleasant air upon him. He notices that there are several others that walk with him besides Ekart Mansour. Up above him the ceiling recedes away it seems and they are in a spacious kind of airy darkness. The sounds of rushing water begin to rise.

This is real, is it not? And soon I will be on my way. To see my Fatima. My darling Fatima. Tariq quietly sobs thinking of the girl, but even more so regretting the loss of the mantle, as if this garment were the very spirit of his friend, taken yet once again. Now therefore he is truly alone and has eternally failed his friend.

They arrive at a stairwell. A stranger assists him in making his way down for he is without his staff as well. His legs tremble but he has sufficient strength when aided to descend. He is seized by a long and violent fit of coughing and he spits somewhere into the darkness. He feels almost weightless yet motion is still difficult and he can barely find his feet to keep moving.

Thank you, thank you, he weakly mutters. Almost there now, he hears. The sound of rushing water grows stronger. It is everywhere now.

107

Candles illuminate a narrow passage roiling with water. The ceiling is far lower here, uneven, craterous, and sinister. There is no vessel in sight.

The old man looks about at his new companions in the filmy light, toothless, fissured, and emaciated mostly, their heads covered, looking lost, looking hopeful. Over here, calls out Ekart Mansour. The ragged little party steps about a corner where they discover a tributary stream that flows more gently than the rushing waters of the main river. Bobbing in the stream is a large canoe, maybe ten feet long, plain and sturdy. Ekart Mansour stands with his arms wide open but he makes no effort to enter the boat himself. Another man sits in the boat at the stern, eyes pale green instead of blue. Everyone is encouraged to sit low in the boat for safety, so low that it is difficult to see out. When all are seated Ekart Mansour reappears, producing several shawls all crudely made but sufficient to provide a bit of warmth. He leans over, one knee up, the other on the ground, and in this way Ekart Mansour speaks to the people in the boat, including the trembling old man.

"Listen to me. You are about to leave this place. That is what you want. The way begins here. Laval will take you as far as the river flows. Water flows downward. Never upwards. And that is why we can take you out but it is also why you can never find your way back again the same way. Do you understand?" A stolid silence greeted him. "Once you leave, you are not coming back. Including Laval. Once the water ends he cannot carry you with him. You will have to walk. It will still be far but not so very much. I am told by the rare ocean traveler that you can see your destination waiting for you on the horizon. You have all heard that where you are going is a place where the buildings are white and the streets are clean and silent and the fountains and the sky are pure." He scans the mute and quiescent heads. "Hold on. Be safe. You are in good hands with Laval but there are no guarantees. You are not tourists." He points. "The water is swift. After a day or two and much darkness and narrow passages, you will eventually see the light from the outside, the pure sunlight upon a long open plane far away from here.

"Unless of course you arrive there by night. In which case...." And at this he unexpectedly laughs. He flattens and stiffens his hand and he makes it very slowly glide and skiff its way downward. His hand is now the vessel itself planing gently downward and he is like a god from whose hand the vessel is made, the extension of his being. "The water will be calm by the time you see the light. But it will be very rough until then. The darkness will be total at times. So try to sleep. When it is calm you may drink from the water. It is not a sewer. Be grateful. Laval keeps a bag of meal as well. But mostly just sleep. Just try to sleep. Try to eat as little as possible until you see the light and the water is calm. You will be emerging out of the rock and onto the narrow lazy river that flows within sight of your destination. From there you will walk. You should be out of the monsoon by then and away from the sand storms as well, for such phenomena attach themselves excessively to this place like flies attach themselves to carrion.

"You will walk and it may take you up to two days further to reach the city walls. They are open and you will find your way in. You are quite lucky. One day soon, many more of your kind will seek a way out and when that day comes the walls of your beloved may be closed to them. But not to you." He seems to reflect on this and he strokes his beard. "And yet, even if the walls should be closed to you after all, I suspect you would rather spend the rest of your days sitting in peace outside the walls of your beloved then by wandering inside this open wasteland where up until right now this very moment, you have always dwelled." It is lost on every muted face that to sit forever outside the walls of any desert city would presumably mean certain death by thirst, starvation, and exposure to the elements. The old man notices that Ekart Mansour is a young and handsome man. This he had not expected. Mansour smiles and casts his eyes about his meager passengers. "It's not too late to stay behind in the world you already know." But not one passenger really even hears him say this and he offers no one back his investment.

"Lie back and sleep now if you wish." And at this point, Ekart Mansour rises in a single effortless gesture. Slowly he nods. The boat begins to move, gliding as if on air. The river sound rises and the boat suddenly dips and jostles with a creak and a rumble, turning sharply and rising again as it casts itself about the turgid waters. The old man lies on his back wrapped in his shawl, feeling petals of mist settle upon him, utterly unconcerned or touched by the violent motion of the vessel. Soon the motion of the boat is as though nothing at all. Soon he will be asleep. And before he can even finish his thought he is already watching himself as another person, as if once upon a time he had lived as a man named

Tariq, a man who is lost and who still sits alone in the dark on a narrow winding stairwell that has come to a dead end.

This man called Tariq tries to steady his hands which have grown discolored from chill and from stress. Now he inhabits this man once more, watching the purple emaciated hand twitching before him. He has no fear though. For he is no longer this man anymore, even if he once was, even if the man is still there, still staring alone at his own withered hand. The old man opens his eyes in the dark and the river still violently courses yet he is not afraid. He smiles for he is here, taken care of, and on his way to a better place.

Beneath the relentless chant of the river, the old man hears the murmurings and even the laughter of some of his faceless companions. All will yet be right with this world and in the world to come. He closes his eyes again. It is difficult to know whether his eyes are open or closed except by their sensation, for there is total absence of all light. He dreams of the iron works and how the towering plumes of fires soar into the coal black sky. Now they are oddly beautiful to him as he looks back upon them in his mind. For years he labored and lived beneath the depths and he watched others fall all around him. He used to count them as they became withered or broken. Finally he stopped counting.

The water in the mines was abundant but only to cool and mold the iron beast. There were no rivers. One day they released him into the largesse of his wandering retirement. He slept wherever he chose and he dreamed his dreams for free and he ate modestly at whatever chamber was open to him and he could bathe and purify himself in the glowing sulfur ponds, the ones that were mild enough. He lived therefore in a place where all was abundance. But now he was at last on a sacred pilgrimage to a land where suffering was no longer required and where beauty was no longer hidden within its riddle of ugliness. The old man opened his eyes but all was still darkness. The waters were deafening yet all was calm within him and the motion of the vessel was comforting. As he moved his hand tentatively across the bottom of the boat, as if to touch the surface of the present moment upon the roughhewn surface of the vessel, he also touched the hand of another, a bony, warm little hand that held his own and they lay that way, invisible to each other, holding each other's hand.

And the old man finally ceased counting, not realizing he had likely been doing so all along. He felt the warmth of that sweet pathetic

110

hand. Weakly he squeezed it. The old man entered fully into the moment and his mind became blank and there was nothing more but the sound of water and the touch of that hand. It was not long though before he escaped the moment and resumed his thinking, though no longer counting but now watching himself count, viewing himself from outside his body, no longer here on this boat, but once more now witnessing that part of himself that had been left behind on that lonely stairwell. It seemed that this man on that stair had once thought that he could soften these walls by counting mutely upon them, softening his walls into abstractions. The old man is so sad for this man and tells himself that he is no longer there, that he is no longer him and he feels instead for the touch of that other hand, the hand of another, and he squeezes that hand and the other hand squeezes back. And so there is only the touch of another's hand and that is his world now and the world is ordered and there is the water and the motion all around him. So this is the way to another place. And he talks in soothing tones to himself in his sleep for a very long time.

In his dreams he is forever about to board the very vessel he has already boarded. Often he is alone. The vessel is by turns splendid and decrepit. He speaks to his daughter and weeps at the memory of her essential beauty. At last he finds himself in an endless body of roiling water, the silver angry skies lording above, and everything is merciless and terrifying yet he is not afraid. He had heard of this place, this causeless sea, a vast plane beyond all comprehension, a well-spring of being that people spoke of with reverence yet disbelief. There was no more need for fear, he saw that now. Fear was pointless for everything had already been settled and all that remained including himself was utterly indestructible. The old man ceases his struggles and floats upon the infinite plane of existence, liberated and at one with everything.

He awakens rudely as yet another wave from the ocean reveals itself as the underground river splashing upon him and he hears himself coughing and he is surrounded in the dark by faceless companions who hold him and who help him to finally sit up. He is the last to awaken. The vessel finally settles and the others are laughing and clapping. The old man trembles and someone speaks to him and he cannot understand for they seem to speak another language. He tries to speak but all he can do is wheeze and he ends up coughing again.

111

The waters are calm but he is not. Someone hands him a shawl and so does someone else and the old man is shivering and so he gratefully accepts these kindnesses. They wrap him in the shawls and speak to him in their gibberish tongue. All is silent for a moment. Then they resume speaking and laughing and the old man works his mouth and smacks his lips but nothing comes out and he decides it doesn't matter.

The darkness has softened and a dim metal light casts a feint glow upon the vessel and its passengers. He can see now that they are floating in a far more spacious passage, the cave ceiling still raw yet no longer bearing down upon them. The waters are calm at last and the row man whose name he has forgotten lightly rows and guides the nexus forward. Someone offers him an earthen cup of water and he drinks and the water is sweeter and lighter than anything he has ever tasted before. The old man trembles and feels weak and insubstantial but he is happy. He feels something towards these strangers in the boat with him. As the darkness continues to soften, the people in the boat who are all talking and laughing now begin to sing. Their voices are pinched and toneless and utterly beautiful. The old man is happy and weak. He cannot name the feeling, the kinship he feels towards these gentle strangers who laugh and sing and are unabashed in their hope for what lies ahead.

Indeed at the first moment of that first light, they laugh and sing all the louder at the distant yet unmistakable glittering point that finds its way towards them. They nudge him and it is clear to him that they mean for him to look.

With an effort greater than he would have guessed for him to take he turns his head and indeed he must squint at the sharpness of light that shafts its way with growing presence upon the vessel. His bones feel hollow and his throat is dry and everything within him feels like it is sinking. And though his body is leaving him, he resists the compelling urge to descend forever beneath the ocean waves. He listens to the busy chatter and the laughter of his kinsman and he continues to look upon the light. One last time he witnesses that terrible black and purple hand scything across his view. It is the man who was lost in the earthen stairwell calling out to him but the old man invites its ghost to join him here instead to witness this joy and this light.

Everything is the light. Soon they will see their precious destination in the palpable distance and then they will surely be at peace forever. The old man smiles though it takes all that he has. Even the thought of his precious daughter falls away.

At last he feels himself dissolving and with that he gently surrenders himself, entering fully at last into the light.

∞

SIX MILLION YEARS LATER

One day, while sitting on the toilet, Hillekend became so heavy-lidded, so meditative, that he completely forgot who he was and where he was and so therefore he fell into a reverie for precisely six million years. One minute he was ether, the next he could hear again with his own ears the gentle, white noise of his electric fan, still running. The incense, of course, had burned out long ago, and had gathered much dust. The room seemed very much the same, although it took his senses a few moments to re-adjust, to see his bathroom as small and cozy, instead of vast and infinitely variegated. He stared at the wine and cream colored wall paper, with little flower designs, the door, just a foot from his right arm, with the little picture of the puppy and the street urchin with the huge soulful eyes. He curled his toes into the thick, furry carpet, matted with age. It had been the peaceful sound of the fan that had put him into such his trance. Not that he was complaining. He felt, on the contrary, more refreshed than he could remember feeling for, well, at <u>least</u> six million years, if not quite a bit longer. Still, such a long time in the bathroom did tend to mess up ones work schedule, throwing all kinds of research out of line, perhaps rendering it completely useless. Ah, but then again, he mused, impermanence, maya, that was the main lesson he needed to learn again and again. So good show for the fan after-all. The mountain will still be there, or would it have been eroded completely by wind and rain. Could he now climb it at last upon his little white legs. A wonder it was that the Tartars had not yet found their way to his door. Well, what of it. There were no more Tartars, anyway. Accept. Onward.

He reached for his thick, square, black bi-focals, still on the marble sink next to the soap dish. A little greasy but he could rinse them. His faucet moaned and out came at first a viscus, ammonia substance, so he let it run for a few minutes until the water finally ran clear again. The bathroom door was stuck, understandably so, but upon his third effort it opened with a sound of snapping tree bark under foot. It opened with a whine. What a relief. He began to take stock of his

114

things, his files, his papers, his ink pens, his books, his crystals collection, his house-plants, even his cactus, were all long dead and shriveled. All of these things were so strange yet familiar to him. Finally, he ventured to step outside to see if Mount Veda was still there. The front door, made of logs and cork-board, gave him even more trouble than the bathroom door, because it was blocked by a good four feet of earth layer. Fortunately, it opened inward. His heart leaped at the sight.

It was late winter, probably early March he guessed, and it was just that remarkable time of morning when the eastern sky was coal-hot red with the sun, so huge and near to the earth, yet so cool, while the western sky was still full of stars. Stars he had never seen before, constellations out of alignment, even Orion's belt, loosened, his paunch spilling over, giggling, dizzy stars, that tilted further towards the planet than he ever remembered. The earth at his feet was black and wet, etchy patched with frost. Blackened trees, gnarled boughs screaming silently, enveloped his cottage, twisting and rooting over his shingles, a gigantic trunk fallen a perilous few feet from his door, a great twisted root fingering toward him, while the walls were covered with a thick coat of moss, lichens, and mushrooms. Such a nuisance. The forest was full of silent, twisted trees, adorned with knobby proboscises and scars. Beyond the forest, rising from behind a verdant hill, great garments of mist hid from view the sight of Mount Veda, which had grown darker and taller by perhaps a half a mile, flanked by shoulders of massive craggy peaks stretching away on either side. A very light fall of snow and ash made its way to earth. Hillekind watched the sun rise, the return of the great tomato from the east. He began to rummage again his moldy room, objects delicate as dust-bunnies, looking for the most well preserved, least yellowed writing paper beneath volumes of mulchy atlases, now long obsolete. When at last he found a few scraps of usable paper and a dull pencil, he sat upon the couch, bit the end of the pencil as if to carefully weigh his next words, and then began to write, scarcely bothering to notice whether his words joined the page: I have this instinct to remember who I am, although I know that I am already gone, and soon, perhaps any minute, I will leave this earth and leave not a single trace of me. It will be spring soon. The earth has already begun to thaw. A fine time for me to return to earth. I do not know what year it is but, of course, it does not matter. Nothing matters, really. I had once been so fond of exactitudes and ways of measuring things. But there is no more need for measuring anything. There never was.

How many countless times has every tree in this forest lived and died, how many times did every particle of the mountain outside my door replace itself. While I was in the bathroom. Everyone I ever knew is long dead, of course, their many descendants, all the genes of their kind, gone, as well as every tree nurtured from their dust, and every seed and root from every tree, all gone, many times over. And how many cells in my body have died and been reborn even in the time it has taken me to write down these very words. Ah, but I am already dead anyway. Dead and blissful, too. It is all good. Most of my life had been devoted to research and learning. What of all our science and transforming technology, it is all gone as though it were never here. And the beautiful earth has survived, it gives me joy I say to see it. It has returned to its primordial state, divine and untouched by any presumption of human knowledge.

I grew up in a large mid-western city, the only child of a Catholic mother and an ascetic Protestant father. Each made their own private devotions to their own God. Mother had her own private shrine in a nook in the little dining room, with rosaries, flower petals, fragrant berry colored petals, a cinnamon candle lit at night, and a letter sized framed portrait of the mythical meek and mild Jesus. I remember well her devout and tidy alcove. Father was silent. He read the paper every night in the den, like clockwork, from eight until nine, and he folded his paper without a crease into perfect trifolds. Ten minutes of silence in his chair, then bed. Every morning at six he left home for work in the print-shop in his gray vest and blinding white shirt, with all the solemnity of a nuclear physicist charged with perfecting the bomb. Eventually I inherited his discipline, his respect for hard facts, yet I was also touched by my mother's mysticism. The world was filled with spirits and seraphim, and watchful eyes, the unseen, all of which I now understand terrified my father.

At school I was despised, pasty faced, with a sour face and hatchet nose. With my dangly frame and coke-bottle glasses I closely resembled a Mongoloid, save for my clear eyes and better formed head. I did poorly at school until I went to a third rate city college and earned my way mopping cafeteria floors and stacking books at the local library. I was always a voracious reader and read books with a greater possessive thrill than most boys coveted young girls, and with far greater success, too. I began to excel at all the sciences, especially mathematics and physics, and was accepted and excelled first at the local state college, and then a graduate school of national repute. I was fascinated also by history and sociology, anthropology and psychology. I got good grades here too, but in truth I understood not one word of it. It was both my passion to stay in school as well as to avoid at all costs any exposure to the rest of the world. Becoming a research fellow, hidden from view in a laboratory became my only ambition, which I achieved upon obtaining my doctorate, and continued for the next thirty years. I became quite venerable and revered, publishing when required, my eccentric appearance and reclusiveness were now mistaken for admirable devotion to my work. Then one day I became truly devout. I had reached the limits of my faith in understanding the material world. The more I probed the outer reaches of the universe, the inner reaches of the nucleus, the more I knew that the universe had truly stumped me and that to go deeper I needed to know what every simple heart already knows. I could always probe deeper like a straight line into the womb of knowledge but I no longer took any joy from it and it only seemed to take me farther and farther from anything I could hold on to.

One day before dawn I left the laboratory and came here. I started growing plants. I built my own generator and was able to easily take care of my needs. A rusty pick-up took me the forty miles each way to the closest store twice a month for batteries, seeds, and food. I planted flowers and tomatoes and carrots and roots. I nurtured plants and vines and leafy things in a clearing around my house before the forest. My garden became my primary work, my solitude, my exploration. I had once read a good deal of travel stories, epic poems by the ancients, myths of creation. I began to write poetry and make up stories a child would about all my flowers and even my vegetables, and the trees and the rocks and the streams and even the bracken and dead things on the forest floor, and finally the sky. I knew these stories and myths were as intimate knowledge as any I could obtain through quantitative research. I observed. I actually saw. These maidens, these warriors and saints, and wanderers and priests, and artists and jugglers, and dancers and mystics all, they all live on in my garden, my forest, the earth, the sky. Finally, every myth and story ran together and I fell silent both inward and out. I sat for hours at a time, then days at a time upon great rocks overlooking

117

the valley. I tried to climb the mountain, but I hadn't the physical strength. As I grew older I watched the mists of morning from my porch, barely any further. My garden died. Lack of care. It returned to the earth.

The most carefully maintained part of my estate was my bathroom. I had always known peace in the bathroom, the toilet. It had been a place of safety in my childhood, photos of beatific saints on the wall. Not the violent hospital white or urine yellow that make many bathrooms a place of functional horror. Instead, our bathroom was the most human room in our house, and rightly so. It is a place of refuge, and a place where the sacred rite of cleansing the body, both the outer body and the inner body, is consecrated. What better place to enjoy a spiritual epiphany as well, the body naturally relaxed, complex yoga postures unnecessary. I always did have a quirk about white fan noise, even with the sounds of nature around me. The sssssssshhhhhhh! eternal sound, the perfect noise, the stream without water, without change, ever controlled. Hillekin looked up from his work seeing nothing. Glasses misted over. He lowered his head and concluded. It's time for me to go now. It's time for me to remember where I've been since I last went to the bathroom. It's time for me to return to the earth, to the sky. I'm going back to my garden.

And with that Hillekin effortlessly climbed outside again, the sky a luminescent pale green and pink, the earth crisp, moist, and alive. Mount Veda, snow-capped, evoking a rarified wind more peaceful than a bathroom fan, towered peacefully before him. He nodded, smiled. And before he could close his eyes he was dust and his house as well and his bathroom and his fan and all his papers and his books and every trace of Hillekin and of man gathered in a wind that never moved, untouched by any human mind or need or desire.

Edan Benn Epstein lives in Southern California. He can be contacted at ebepstein@sbcglobal.net. His novels include Empty Sky (1997), Subterranean Green (2011), Fog (2012), The Anteater (2014) and Afternoon of the Faun (2015). His sixth novel, The Rite of Spring, the epic yet intimate story of four dysfunctional siblings and four generations careening through life from the present day until the unrecognizable world of 2080, will be available in 2017. **For further updates, like us on Facebook at Edan Benn Epstein.**

AVAILABLE NOW ON AMAZON! **THE ANTEATER - an existential thriller.**

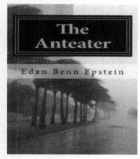

The Anteater, Epstein's fourth novel, follows the hopes, fears, and secrets of seven men working for a third rate messenger service in Los Angeles in 1985. Over the course of three days in November, a perfect storm – both literal and emotional – changes their lives forever. Magic intertwines with grim reality in a tale of deep inner longing forever just one step ahead of existential checkmate. Integrating seven stories, all haunted by the city scape of 1980s Los Angeles, The Anteater *"delves into areas of the human psyche that fiction rarely explores." "A spiritually redemptive act"* **$12.95 in paperback on Amazon.com. (296 pages) Only $2.99 on Kindle.**

AVAILABLE NOW ON AMAZON! **FOG** - *An idyllic tale of mayhem set in the California Redwoods.*

Fog
An idyllic tale of mayhem set
in the California Redwoods

Edan Benn Epstein

Ari Fisher lives the perfect life in the most beautiful place on earth. As the semester ends at the college where he teaches part time, Ari has but one unexpected task to perform; to entertain one of his school's most important donors. In an escalating game of cat and mouse with his charming and unexpected new adversary, Ari's life threatens to come unraveled over the course of a single evening as his inner demons are suddenly unleashed. **Only $8.95 in paperback on Amazon. (154 pages)** *Only 99 cents on Kindle!*

A PREVIEW from beginning of FOG:

December

The road worker from the county was the first to notice that something was terribly wrong. Fog had lifted sufficiently to see the road, but not what lay beyond. Or below. A seasoned road worker or cop could see the black marks, the displaced rocks, could smell the leaking fuel and carburetor smoke. There were no guard rails on this stretch of Highway 1. The road snaked its way against the ocean, ten miles north of Klamath, at least a mile from the nearest habitation.

The county worker suspected that a car had sailed over the cliff during the night and had crashed below. Every year or so, this was bound to happen. Everyone's afraid of the Tsunami, ignorant or dismissive of the real risk out here.

Eventually, everyone would be able to see it, the disaster below. But even then it would be a sonovabitch to remove it, even the body, for the car would be impaled against the rocks, abutting a jagged cliff, buffeted by the constant waves. Until the moment it sinks altogether. If it's still there, it's overtime pay for sure, he thought, with little enthusiasm. He picks up his radio to make the call.

The following May

Rain persisted for the third straight night. It fell from the unseen places, from the mists and from the flat gray sky. It turned the rare barren slopes into mud slips that choked the narrow hillside lanes overlooking the invisible ocean. It fell by turns in mists and torrents, flooding the trails, sluicing down gutter ways.

The rain slowed Ari's progress towards his home, two miles north of Trinidad harbor, through a winding verdant road and onto a flat dirt lane. Even at close range, his home and his manicured lawn was hidden by the hanging wet canopy of branch and leaf. Ari felt witness to yet immune from the elements. They were his to enjoy from his comfortable arm chair, watching the rainwater slide down his window, drench his lawn, and fill his ears. The sounds grew louder.

During an average commute it takes an hour for Ari to reach the college south of Eureka. This is without traffic; but there almost never is any traffic, except where the 101 passes directly through the streets of Eureka, a town that persists in disappointing him in its ugly junkiness. Even the Victorian style buildings downtown have a mean, crowded, and forlorn appearance.

Ari escapes Eureka and heads out on 101 south, past the open green fields to a barely noticeable turn out for the college where he teaches, hidden in its own gentle tree laden world. He doubts he will ever teach at the larger, more prestigious university in Arcata. But this was what he always wanted; a modest yet respectable teaching job conveniently located at the idyllic ends of the earth. That's what Humboldt County was, at least for him; the convenient end of the earth, Brigadoon covered in mists. The hotter the inland frying was during summer, the foggier and colder it persisted in Trinidad and Patrick's Point, but also in Arcata, Orick, Klamath, and far to the north Eureka's smaller, evil twin, Crescent City, and so on along the craggy Redwood coast.

Humboldt County lives between the grasp of the Redwood giants on one side and the shivering gray salty sea on the other. Highway signs warned of possible tsunamis. Crescent City had suffered damage to its harbor and there were eight recorded deaths in 1964, significant for a town of barely a thousand people back then. In 2011, after the cataclysmic quake in Japan, Crescent City was hit again, though not as fiercely. Still, there was one recorded death; that of a foolhardy individual who was swept out to sea while attempting to video tape the event.

When returning home Ari glimpses the bottomless white blanket of endless fog, the ocean evident only from the smell of salt and sperm; Ari's thoughts turn to imagining the poor schmuck whose idle lark turned to panic and struggle and then despair as he likely realized that his very life was imperiled. Even worse was the probable realization that his entire existence culminated in a singular, futile instant of ultimate loss. People often seemed to lose their lives in the most ludicrously frightening ways.

Ari shook the images away. He considered that an irrational part of him expected to be protected by the surrounding mists and fog and rain, that he lived - comfortably now – beyond not just physical threats, but psychological and emotional ones as well. A finger of misty fog crept onto the road as if to greet him.

The next day, Thursday, was uncharacteristically warm and sunny, though rain was predicted again for that night. Ari stoically proctored his finals. Both his classes were sections of Introduction to Cost Accounting. He had already taught this class so many times with so little variation that he knew and anticipated without even thinking about it, every single point, every example, and certainly every joke (few and weak as they were) for every single lecture of this course as well as for all the courses he taught. There were even times when it felt like he had been teaching in a black out and he had little recollection of a morning or an evening. Once or twice, he had even experienced himself "coming to" in the middle of a class. He would lose his place and stood looking at the white board, hands in pockets, trying not to let on. Thoughtfully, he would stroke his chin and look at the book, look out archly at his students, smile, and pick up perfectly from wherever he had left off.

He was engaging and he knew it, when he was fully present. And he supposed he was almost exactly the same when he wasn't. When he was "on" he was helpful, useful, charming, and funny. He energized young minds to embrace business and to go forth and reshape the fluid, sustaining network of business and global wealth. Then there were other days when all of felt pointless and effete, merely abstract fundamentals that fell like toy ghosts upon bovine intellects, listless and unambitious cyber surfers, occupiers of cheap seats at a well-manicured, third rate institution. The best he hoped for on such days – like today – was a polite laugh and a couple of hot and vulnerable looking young women in the class.

Not that he was actually ever going to make a move on any of them. He agreed that moving forward he needed to keep his private appetites as separate from work as possible. Except, of course, for that one time. Or maybe two, if you counted the grown woman who came to see him after she graduated. Everyone knew about the "grown woman", for he had dutifully let the administration know. They appreciated his candor, if not his choices.

No one knew about the other one. No one would ever know. It was wrong and he knew it. And so he vowed never to repeat such behavior.

Ari had what he had characterized as a complicated relationship with his boss, Clarence "Bud" Cameron, the Dean of the Business Department. Cameron had actually told Ari quite often that he admired and valued his teaching skills and methods, as well as his reliability and timeliness when it came to his attendance, grading, and general adherence to college policies. Nonetheless, Ari felt that Cameron, an otherwise kindly, avuncular figure, was generally cool towards him. Though it had never been discussed openly, Ari was certain that it had to do with his disclosed affair with Catherine Lessor. But instead of expressing his disappointment directly, Cameron instead chose to nudge Ari about "stepping up" - just a little bit, he said – outside of the classroom, for the welfare of the department and for the college. Ari was sure. More than once, Cameron reminded Ari, that "we pay you a full time salary, with benefits, for a part time job. You work three days a week, eight months a year. You're not getting rich, of course, but it's not a bad life, with a strong wage in a low price county. It's not unreasonable for us to ask that you help us once in a while on business that helps this school, and therefore, you as well". Something like that.

But Cameron never actually asked him to do anything, outside of showing up at a dinner once in a while. As for more responsibilities, Ari thought he might get to be the faculty advisor for the student accounting club. He was a popular instructor, after all. But no. Dirk Hoth had a lock on that. Did Cameron expect Ari to *ask* for work? He didn't think so. So therefore this was all about Catherine Lessor.

He walked into Cameron's outer office, a shared space with wood paneling. About five minutes late. This meeting was all that stood between him and going home where he could work on grading. He had a lot of work to do, but was planning on taking the night off, this being the last night of school and he had until Monday to finish the goddamn grades. Maybe he'd pick up a movie or two, listen to the rain. If he got bored, there was a woman in Smith River he might call. Maybe he'd see her tomorrow night, Friday night, after an honest day's work, grading.

"Hi Janie," he said, greeting the department secretary. He sat down, expecting Cameron to keep him waiting.

"Go on in, Professor Fisher. He's expecting you." Only Janie called him, Professor. He was only an Instructor. Cameron was leaning back in his swivel chair on the phone, but he quickly wrapped up. "Frank, I'll call you back later." Ari recognized the name of someone from the business office. "Ari, glad to see you. Have a seat." He came from around his desk and took a chair closer to Ari. Even with all the supposed budget cuts, how come Bud Cameron had a larger office with what looked like his own secretary? Was this Harvard? "Glad the semester's over?"

"Oh, you know, it'll be nice to be completely loose for a bit. It's not like it's so grueling, Bud."

"Yes, yes, that's right," Cameron agreed. "That's right," he repeated. "Yes…we have it pretty good, I'd say." Ari sensed Cameron might as well have said, *you* have it pretty good.

"Yes, I do. But I was thinking of taking on that fund accounting class, if you still want me to."

"Maybe…Good to know. But I need your help with something else, more immediate, actually."

"Really? Tell me. The semester is over, like you said," Ari pointed out, instantly wishing he had kept that needless observation to himself.

"That's right," Cameron agreed, impatiently. "But the school has expenses and needs all the time."

"True!" Ari piped up.

"Of course, we're funded by the state, but you know very well that the state budget is in the shit hole right now. Education is being cut right and left, even though it hasn't affected us in the business department quite as much. Now we've always been grateful for alumni and other private donations, but now more so than ever. Otherwise," he said, leveling Ari with a look, "We may need to start cutting classes, or even non-tenured faculty, Ari."

"Right." That was a direct, goddamn threat, Ari thought.

"Don't worry, Ari," Cameron said, leaning back, his chair creaking. "I'm not asking you to donate money," he said, smiling. Ari did not smile back. "I do need your help though in collecting it."

"Sure. Just tell me what you need me to do."

"Really, Ari, it's the simplest thing in the world. We've already done the 'telethon' if you will. All I am going to ask you to do is what you do best and enjoy the most, Ari."

"Teach a class?"

"Take a donor out to dinner. A woman donor, Ari. It will be a very charming evening. We have all but secured a very sizable check, make that *very* sizable check. It will be enough to guarantee retention of our part time non-tenured faculty, like you, Ari."

"I see."

"She's a widow. Her grandson graduated from her two years ago. He was to matriculate into HSU, but then he died suddenly. Tragically."

"In the tsunami?" Ari offered, pointing upwards, to Crescent City.

"Is that funny, Ari?"

"No. Probably not, Bud. What happened?" Ari asked, trying to sound sincere and sober now.

"He drove his car off Highway One, over the cliffs. Last December. You might have heard about that. It made the news."

"Oh, God. How horrible," He remembered the incident.

"Mrs. Ng is in town through Saturday --"

"Mrs Ing?"

"Yes, Victoria Ng. She's originally from Vietnam, I'd guess, as so many of our students are, nowadays."

126

"Yes."

"Of course. Those of us who involved in the Founders' activities have heard of her." Those of us who play team and who give a shit about our school have all heard of her, is what he might have said, is what Ari decided. And he would have had so much more respect for Bud if in fact he really had spoken his mind like that. He let it pass.

"The delicate part's already done," Cameron went on. "She came to us. We met with her. It's a done deal. But…you know as a goodwill gesture, as a class act, we took the hint that since she was at loose ends this Friday, we offered to find her someone to….accompany her."

"Tomorrow?"

"Yes. You catch on."

"What do you mean, 'accompany'?"

"Ari, it's nothing. Take her out to dinner. Take her to Turendotte, on our dime, of course. That's all. She's an intelligent woman. You should have no lack of conversation."

"How do you know I don't already have plans?"

"Do you?" Read a book. Watch a movie on his home big screen. Watch the rain. Cyber troll for bored and lonely women pining in Quincy, Fortuna, Smith River, even Weed. Driving was no problem.

"No, Bud. Just grading papers. Lots of them"

"Take a break from that."

"Well, in fact, I am planning on spending the day with my son on Saturday, Bud. He's leaving the country for two years on a Peace Corps mission."

"Ah yes, that's right. They still have that going on, the Peace Corps. Good for him. Outstanding."

"So that's why I need to finish my grading tomorrow."

"Makes sense. It's Simon. Right?"

"Simon. That's correct." At that moment, Ari did not like the idea of Bud Cameron even knowing his son's name.

"That's wonderful, Ari. Of course it is a very long time to be without your boy."

"Yes."

"He's probably just a bit younger than my son."

"Must be nice to have a son who's a cop."

127

"You think? I worry about him, you know. Even though he's not going far away, like Simon." Ari merely nodded and grunted, restraining himself from pointing out that there was likely little danger to a CHP officer here in Humboldt County. Cameron continued. "Anyway, I'm really sorry about the last minute notice, Ari, I grant you that. But our donor, she actually requested you specifically, young man. Mrs. Ng. I would have picked you regardless, but now I really need your help."

"She picked me?"

"You were her grandson's favorite instructor. Leon Ng."

"Oh."

"I'm not surprised about that. But I really need you to play team on this."

"I had a feeling you'd say that."

"Did you? Is there a reason you can't go to your office right now, or even go home and just bang these out, the paper's you're grading, today and tomorrow morning? And Sunday? Grades aren't due until Tuesday morning, you know that."

It'll be damned hard if I decide to hike up around Orick for a day or two, Ari thought. "No. Probably not. It's just a surprise, is all. I suppose you feel I owe it to the team." Cameron just looked at him. "Well…..Bud, I agree."

"Good. Glad to hear you say that."

"So…fine…so what am I supposed to do exactly?"

"Be charming. Not necessarily too charming, if you know what I mean," and Cameron winked at him with good humor. You mean, don't fuck her, Bud, is what he thought. "Mrs. Ng will be expecting you to pick her up where she's staying at the Comfort Suites near the airport. It's all arranged."

"I know where it is."

"Just take her to dinner and charge it to us. Whatever you want. Take her to Turendotte, or whatever your favorite restaurant is. Listen to her wax on about her dead son."

"You're quite the sentimentalist, Bud."

"Just be charming and interested, a good listener, and all that."

"Alright. I guess I'm flattered. Anything else?"

128

Cameron just looks at him for a moment. "This is very important to us, Ari. This is not a difficult task, I think, but we're really counting on you. We know you won't let us down."

Ari was back on the road by three. He loved the serene near empty outer parking lot near the campus entrance, and he loved the conceit that he had found a place on the edge of the world; a comfortable one of course, with indoor plumbing, lighting, and heating. He looked up at the tall placid trees that flanked every part of the campus. There were twenty seven hours left before he had to dispatch his duty of babysitting some self-important elder donor who no doubt would spend the entire evening eulogizing her beloved grandson.

Ari had just turned 52, was divorced, unencumbered, self-sufficient, and self-determined. He became a CPA, the fastest, cheapest, safest way to obtain a prestigious and lucrative career; no law school, no medical school, no graduate studies at all. He passed the exam in two tries straight out of school. Ari was considered handsome and rugged, premature gray and bright green eyes. He put in his two years at a then Big Eight CPA firm, enough to get his requisite experience to obtain his license. Ari was asked to stay on for a third year, but left instead to work for a regional firm before finally leaving public accounting to go work internally for a large engineering firm. He climbed as high as manager, right below the CFO and settled there with a good salary, great benefits, and as much responsibility as he wanted. Then he married a sensible, sharply attractive woman who worked in quality assurance, one with a respectable income of her own.

Sabrina seemed well enough adjusted apart from a tendency to talk a great deal about her college days as a dancer and how she might have pursued it further but she did not want a life of living on the edge and so she became an engineer instead. She hated it but it did impress her family and made her independent, and as a member of quality.

Whenever she spoke of it at a dinner party over her third glass of Chardonnay, animated and loud, there was supportive laughter all around, for she was being ironic and self-depreciating. Ari was quite aware that whereas Sabrina pointed out every single time he told a story more than once, she herself had no clue how many times she did the same thing, glass in hand, but that was something that he was never going to tell her.

His job was easy and he and Sabrina purchased a large and comfortable home in the early nineties, outside of San Jose, which appreciated greatly during the Clinton and early Bush years. Prosperity and innovation had swept most of the nation. Crime went down. At the time of their home purchase, the Russians had become allies, even if precariously so, while freedom seemed to sweep new part of the world from eastern Europe to central Asia. All was well except in a few obscure parts of the world, like Rwanda, Kosovo, Chechnya, Somalia, Congo, North Korea, Iraq, Afghanistan, China, Burma, Syria, Yemen, Lybia, India, Columbia, Mexico, and the invisible desperate millions even in the United States. And the list, Ari realized, could be extended indefinitely. Yes, it would be enough for him to be able to name just a few of these countries by name to show that he cared and to impress others at campus mixers of his worldliness. Sabrina and Ari had earned tax savings by giving regularly to charities both within and outside the United States. Ari, on his own, decided to continue the practice.

Their son Simon was about to join the Peace Corps. He would soon be on his way to help build school houses and teach poor Guatemalan children. Ari was genuinely proud of his son, but also found him a bit idealistic or maybe just on the make for adventure.

Ari cultivated hobbies like hiking, canoeing, and camping, though Sabrina did not share in these. (They did, however, ski and play tennis together.) With his college friend, Albert, the lone remaining vestige of his young adult buddies, he went backpacking and fly fishing in Oregon at least once a year. These were manly occupations that compensated for the lucrative, but admittedly sterile work he had chosen.

He fondly remembered his early sex life with his good looking, responsive wife, which was easy and efficient. Such memories now often aroused anger which in certain strange moments heightened his solitary arousal. Someone else was fucking her now.

When Sabrina had brought up the subject of children, Ari had been hesitant and wanted to wait, if only a couple of years, hoping secretly to stretch the time frame indefinitely. At first, his wife had gone along with his wishes but it was clear that she was not happy.

All of that changed when he and Albert went hiking one weekend in the Sierras. They were higher up the mountain than they had ever been, and they were now well above the snow level, for there had been a late snow in June that year. The hike had gone well until the tiniest moment of absent mindedness when Ari stepped upon a slick piece of ice that he had taken for snow. The slip and fall seemed to happen in slow motion, yet Ari was unable to correct himself or even to comprehend that his body was out of control. He slid feet first, face down in the snowy slope. His descent was finally stopped by a boulder and cushioned by a snow bank. Ari raised his head, confused by the shouting above. A long time seemed to have passed. He managed to look up and estimate that he was maybe fifty feet from the trail. So he raised his arm, his fist, to signify that he was alright. Albert was still speaking. What? "Don't move, Ari. Don't move! Not yet," he was saying. Albert assiduously instructed him to climb straight up, if he could, digging into the snow, looking ahead to avoid any ice. Slowly.

At first, it didn't seem as if he was making any progress. The last few feet to the trail were the most harrowing. Straight up it seemed. Ari could barely feel his hands anymore. Albert coached him towards a a place where Ari could get his grip. But then he began to slip again his breath caught in his throat, hot crystals of snow and ice mashing into his face. And then just for an instant, Ari held the intrusive suggestion in his head to simply let go and tumble into the abyss, to sleep. He wondered if he would even feel a thing. Albert's voice snapped his attention back to his task. Fear gripped him once more as he still could not feel his hands. "Don't you take me down with you, you bastard!" Albert barked, but he didn't sense any real fear in his friend's voice. Ari managed to sling a leg over the trail and he rested, trying to catch his breath.

131

Almost miraculously, it seemed, Ari had neither twisted nor mangled any limbs. Apart from his hands tingling and burning and his jeans being thoroughly soaked, he was okay. Soon, the two of them reached a fork in the trail which they followed downwards, quickly descending below the snow line. They made it back to the car three hours later as evening was falling. Ari was exhausted and sore.

"Remember when I shouted at you up there, not to move? After you fell, I mean," Albert asked him.

"Yeah. I think that rings a tiny little bell. What happened?"

"Well I'm glad you didn't ask me about it at the time. But had you slid two or three more feet to your right, you would probably have sailed right off the cliff."

Ari looked at him and looked back out at the defrosting front window. "That's what I figured," he said. In his mind, he profusely thanked his friend, yet he remained quiet. Ari thought he might well owe Albert his life. And yet he vaguely resented Albert, because he had slipped and Albert had not and he felt foolish. "Well what was the point of telling me now?" he muttered. But he gave his friend a sheepish grin so as not to offend him. His slip had embarrassed him, but so did his resentment. He certainly did not share with Albert his surreal moment of longing to fall into the abyss.

He mentioned nothing whatsoever about his slip on the mountain with his wife. Following the incident, however, Ari thought about how much ordinary danger he routinely survived; momentary cell phone distractions on the highway, narrowly avoiding high speed collisions; stepping out from his car onto a busy thoroughfare and feeling the carbon wind of a passenger bus narrowly missing him; or even inadvertently pointing the plastic cork of a champagne bottle at himself, the cork bouncing sharply off his head, inches from exploding forever through his eye. Seconds and inches between life and death, between being physically whole and traumatically maimed; these were the conveniently forgotten pivots haunting him in the days following the hiking incident.

11/9/2017

Mark,

It's a joy working together my sister.

Welcome to my mom.

You are welcome to my life

50081163R00080

Made in the USA
Middletown, DE
26 October 2017